Hip hip hoorays for the *Kni*

'Absolutely hilarious nonsen
them for spelling my name wi
that's how funny it is.' Louie Stowell

'Sublimely funny and seriously entertaining,
this is the ideal way to get your youngsters
hooked on reading. . . and medieval mischief!'
Lancashire Evening Post

'**What a hero! What a
story! Sublime daftness
on every page.**'
Jeremy Strong

'I love these books so
much! *Mr Gum* levels of
weird and brilliant.'
Jo Nadin

'Probably the funniest book I've ever read.
A masterclass in silliness!'
Gary Northfield, author of *Julius Zebra* series

'A ridiculously appealing story . . . wacky, original,
fantastic and funny, it's so good you'll have to read
it for yourself!' *School Librarian*

'Brimming with ludicrous magic and
fizzing with irresistible comedy.'
Peter Lord

'As if Hans Christian Andersen had cornered
you in a pub and got his own yarn in the
wrong order, or The Brothers Grimm had
squeezed up next to you with a Tupperware
box of home-made sandwiches on a long
coach journey.' Stewart Lee, comedian

'Dazzlingly silly and brilliant fun. Conrach
Matt Brown Library
01-2228344

KNIGHT SIR LOUIS

AND THE CAULDRON OF CHAOS

GUPPY BOOKS

KNIGHT SIR LOUIS AND THE CAULDRON OF CHAOS
is a GUPPY BOOK

First published in the UK in 2024 by
Guppy Books,
Bracken Hill,
Cotswold Road,
Oxford OX2 9JG

978 1 916558 274

1 3 5 7 9 10 8 6 4 2

Papers used by Guppy Books are from well-managed
forests and other responsible sources.

GUPPY PUBLISHING LTD Reg. No. 11565833

A CIP catalogue record for this book is
available from the British Library.

Typeset in 13½/20 pt Adobe Garamond by
Falcon Oast Graphic Art Ltd, www.falcon.uk.com

Printed and bound in Great Britain by CPI Books Ltd

To Caroline

SO WHO'S IN THIS

KNIGHT SIR LOUIS

The young hero of this tale.
A calm and clear-thinking
champion in a wild, weird
world. The most difficult quests
are entrusted to him. His name
is pronounced 'Loo-ee'.

CLUNKALOT

Clunkie the flying robot horse
is sturdy, brave and true.
He also likes to write, of course,
especially haiku.

BOOK EXACTLY?

HENRIETTA CATALOGUE

A super-smart boar with a love of adventure, mushrooms and adventure. Did I mention she likes adventure? And mushrooms.

PEARLIN

A young, self-taught wizentor (that's a wizard *and* inventor). Always coming up with new and fun ways to use machines and magic.

KING BURT THE NOT BAD

The (mostly) kind and often (not) sensible King of Squirrel Helm who rules from Castle Sideways.

DAVE THE SWORD

A magical sword recycled from a magic mirror. Likes reflecting magical spells, chopping through nasty things, and singing. (Is an awful singer).

MAC N CHEESE

Pearlin's pet dragon with two (fortunately friendly) heads.

MYSTO

The greatest wizentor ever known. Prone to magical accidents. Curently on holiday.

CILLA DA SPELL

A young witch with big ambitions. Has a
brain fizzing and popping with
new ideas and new ways to
become the best-known
witch ever, anywhere,
full stop.

THE CAULDRON OF CHAOS

An ancient, naughty
cauldron who loves
scoffing down money,
gems, gold, silver
and anything
precious. Ha, ha, ho!

CHAPTER WITCH

This is a story about witches.

How do stories about witches usually start? Well, usually . . .

- it's a dark, stormy night
- there are three witches

- on a spooky lump of land called a heath
- with a big cauldron full of a nasty soup made from frogs' toes and newts' eyeballs.

But that isn't how this story begins.

Sorry, you're not in this story.

But don't worry. There are going to be some witches. And there is definitely going to be a big cauldron.

CHAPTER 1

Cilla Da Spell was a witch.

Almost.

She was an apprentice. She had taken her witchery exams, but they still hadn't sent a letter. Had she passed or not?

It was awful having to wait for the results.

She'd been an apprentice for sooooo long. She had spent so much time having to do what she was told by the older witches. She couldn't wait to leave. Yes, she had enjoyed the lessons about spells and magic. But the things they learnt seemed ancient and dull. Where was the new magic?

She had never really clicked with the other

apprentices either. Nobody was mean to her. But they weren't friends either. The others seemed to be content to learn the old spells and nothing more. But Cilla wanted to invent her own spells and potions! She often volunteered for chores. That way she could be on her own and think about her magical ideas. She cleaned the potion bottles, washed and ironed the witches' robes, added sticky cobwebs to the doorways and made sure the stairs were still creaky.

Right now, she was scrubbing out one of the many cauldrons. They were all so battered and blackened. It was back-breaking work. She promised herself that when she made full witch, she'd get herself a lovely brand-new non-stick cauldron. As she worked, she liked to listen to Radio Owl.

Hoooo-doooo! Twit-twoo!

Today's headlines:

King Burt has just returned from an exciting tour of the other kingdoms.

He enjoyed a day at the new fun park, the Big Widget, in the kingdom of Proud Fidget.

He was very impressed by the Republic of Klaptrap's new theme park, Thunderclap Towers.

And finally, he also spent time at the Principality of Plopp's new adventure centre, Top of the Plopps.

Cilla listened with envy. She wished she could be like King Burt. Be her own boss. Do whatever she wanted when she wanted!

Just then, as she scraped the inside of the cauldron with a wire brush, she heard the letterbox clatter. Cilla climbed out of the cauldron and went to the door. There on the ground was a gilt-edged envelope addressed to her. She took off her cleaning gloves and picked up the envelope. She carefully lifted out the letter inside. Slowly but surely, a big smile crossed Cilla's face.

To Cilla Da Spell
Witchery School
Crone Castle
Dismal Wood

7th of the Month of Long Fingernails
(by the New Witch's calendar)

Dear Cilla,

It is with great pleasure that we write to inform you of the
results of your recent examination. You have passed the
Witchery Exam with Distinction.

Congratulations, you are no longer an apprentice. You are
now a fully qualified witch.

Yours sincerely,

Ada Cadabra,
Chief Witch
The Cave of Creepy Crawlies
Board of Witchery Exams
The Swamp of Mists

OH, LETTER! THOU ART MUSIC TO MINE EARS! AT LAST, I BE A TRUE WITCH!

CHAPTER 2

Here is King Burt the Not Bad.

King Burt has just arrived home to Castle

Sideways. You would think that after his tour he'd be bright and breezy. But instead, he was as glum and grumpy as Cilla Da Spell was ecstatic.

'It's so boring here! Why don't I have an amusement park?' he grumbled to himself.

He looked around for his champion knight. Surely Knight Sir Louis, daring adventurer, would have some exciting ideas about how they could get their own fun park built right here outside Castle Sideways!

'Sorry, your majesty,' explained a footman. 'He's busy. He's about to save the world again.'

King Burt shook his head, irritated.

'Typical! Saving the world. Pah! But what about me? I want to have fun!'

CHAPTER 3

And now, an exciting chapter featuring our hero, Knight Sir Louis!

CHAPTER 4

Knight Sir Louis raced through Castle Sideways. A hero was needed! And Louis was ready. He raced down to the stables. He jumped onto the back of his robot horse Clunkalot. He lifted his magic sword Dave in the air and shouted heroically:

FOR THE KINGDOM OF SQUIRREL HELM!

A cheer went up from the castle courtiers. They loved Louis. (They also thought it was about time somebody chose a new name for the kingdom. Squirrel Helm was just too silly. But no one had come up with anything better yet.)

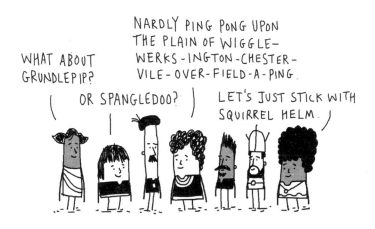

WHAT ABOUT GRUNDLEPIP?

NARDLY PING PONG UPON THE PLAIN OF WIGGLE-WERKS-INGTON-CHESTER-VILE-OVER-FIELD-A-PING.

OR SPANGLEDOO?

LET'S JUST STICK WITH SQUIRREL HELM.

A moment later, Clunkalot leapt into the air, unfurled his robot wings, and they were away. They flew low across the fields, did a loop-the-loop and flew straight down towards the ground. But don't worry, they weren't about to smash into the earth. They flew into a huge crack in the land and then disappeared underground!

Clunkie turned on his headlamp eyeballs to find his way through the underground tunnels. The world around Louis sparkled. Gems of white, green, blue, yellow and red studded the walls of the caves. It was quite beautiful. But Louis wasn't distracted. He had a mission. Deep down under the ground, a clan of invaders was preparing to launch an attack.

No, the invaders were diamonds! Sharp and sparkly living diamonds. Did you know that diamonds are so hard and tough that they can cut through almost anything, including solid rock?

These living diamonds usually kept themselves

to themselves. But long ago, a passing wizard had accidentally dropped a bottle of curses. The bottle smashed on the

ground and the magic potion inside spilt on the soil. The potion had trickled down, down, down, far under the ground for weeks, months, years, centuries . . . until eventually it dripped onto the living diamonds. That's when they turned bad.

Now the diamonds were preparing to head out and take over the world. Nothing would stand in their way. Nothing, except the heroic Knight Sir Louis!

Louis had to act fast. He guessed his sword Dave would be the key to a successful mission.

Dave was a special, magical sword, made from the shards of a magic mirror. His full name was Senator Jibber Jabber Ticket Flick It Sprocket Wicket Dingle David. One of Dave's amazing powers was the ability to repel evil spells.

CELEBRITY SWORD MAGAZINE

EXCLUSIVE INTERVIEW WITH HERO

DAVE THE SWORD!

DAVID IS A ONE-OF-A-KIND SWORD.

MADE BY WORLD FAMOUS WIZENTOR MYSTO!

MADE FROM THE REMAINS OF A MAGIC MIRROR!

WORKING WITH CHAMPION
KNIGHT SIR LOUIS

Dave is the strongest sword
ever made! He can swallow
dragon fire! His magic blade
repels evil spells! Likes to
shout heroic words in battle
like:

HALBADOOR! SUNKYWOT! YANGLEBOOT!

Dave also loves to sing! You'll
love his special voice (if you
are a walrus). If you're not a
walrus, you might want to buy
yourself some earplugs.

Louis, Clunkie and Dave raced down, down, down until suddenly the tunnel opened into a huge cave containing a vast underground lake. Gathered on the shore of the lake was an army of living diamonds.

Louis held up Dave and shouted, 'I come to rid you of your curse! Prepare for battle!'

Dave was ready and excited for the adventure.

CHAPTER 5

The diamonds all had the same thought. FIGHT! They grabbed one another, then spun around and launched themselves into the air. A barrage of diamonds flew towards Clunkie, and Louis had to swing Dave around fast to knock each one away.

TING. CLONG. FINK.

As each diamond hit Dave's blade, each diamond's curse was lifted.

Gradually there were fewer and fewer cursed diamonds and more and more cured diamonds. Then quite suddenly, the battle was over. Hoorah! Louis and Clunkalot landed beside the diamonds at the lake's edge.

'Thank you for your help,' said one of the diamonds gratefully.

'My pleasure,' said Louis. 'I hope I didn't hurt you with my sword.'

'Not at all,' said another particularly sharp and

pointy diamond. 'We're the hardest thing in the world. Nothing dents us!'

'We just hope we haven't hurt your sword,' said another diamond with a blue glow.

Louis smiled and said, 'Oh, Dave's fine, I'm sure.'

And then he turned to look at his sword.

And Dave wasn't fine.

Dave wasn't fine at all.

'Oh no!' said Louis, suddenly concerned for his trusty blade. He turned to Clunkalot. 'Come on, Clunkie. We need to get him fixed as soon as possible!'

And off they flew.

The diamonds watched them go, relieved that they'd been saved. They decided to celebrate the lifting of the evil curse by going for a nice swim in the lake.

Unfortunately, the lake was still polluted with

the potion of curses. All the diamonds became evil again. Once more, they were determined to take over the world.

They started the long, long climb towards the world above.

I WONDER HOW LONG IT WILL TAKE?

ABOUT 30-ISH CHAPTERS, I RECKON.

CHAPTER 6

Cilla Da Spell was a witch. It was official!

She packed her bags and left without even saying a proper goodbye to the older witches who had trained her. She was keen to start witching her own way. She was determined to be the most wonderful witch anyone had ever seen. She had plans to revolutionise witching. Everything the

older witches did was so old-fashioned and boring boring boring! Cilla would show them! Yes! She had real ambition. For starters, there was the matter of where you lived. She wasn't going to live in some creepy old cottage.

Cilla was going to get herself a super-cool house on legs. She was going to get herself a house on chicken legs. Oh yes! And then a mansion on elephant legs. You bet! And then a castle on dinosaur legs! Bring it! But for now, she had to settle for a hut on duck legs.

QUACK!

Cilla was determined to be known across the kingdoms as THE witch to go to for all your magical needs. But what was the special something she would do?

No.

She's going to . . . open a shop!

Perhaps she'll make a fortune.

CHAPTER 7

Meanwhile, in other places, people were losing a fortune. A little bit at a time. Here and there, around the kingdom, things were going missing. A ruby here. A pouch of silver coins there. An emerald on a ring here. A nugget of gold there.

Each time something went missing, there was a cracked, battered and slightly melted cauldron nearby. Nobody paid it much attention.

IS THAT SUPPOSED TO BE THE CAULDRON OF CHAOS?

CAN'T BE.

IT'S JUST A BATTERED OLD BIT OF METAL.

But it was. The cauldron had seen better days, yes. It had been made long, long ago. After many exciting, naughty adventures it had found itself dropped into a lava flow from an erupting volcano. The cauldron's magic protected it from being melted. But when the lava cooled, the cauldron found itself stuck inside hard volcanic stone. It stayed there for a very loooooooonng time. But do you know what's harder than rocks and stone?

1. Ham and Cheese Toasties
2. Lampposts
3. Rain

Slowly but surely, the rain eroded the stone away. After a few centuries the cauldron rolled free and set about repairing itself. If you were ever unlucky enough to get close to it, you might hear its thoughts whispering in your mind.

CHAPTER 8

After Louis' underground adventure, he rushed Dave back to Castle Sideways. He went straight to resident nurse Matron O'Goole. Here is her medical report:

DAVE THE SWORD — MEDICAL REPORT

Ooooo! Ohhhh! Twas a day that had started bright and full of promise. But then, a fog, grey and slow, tumbled across the plains towards the castle. It was as if sadness itself had become a cloud. It wrapped itself around the castle, its knight and most of all, his sword David.

Oooooooh! Poor David lay upon the examination bed, a faraway look in his eyes. What did he see, there in his once shining imagination? The end of his famed adventures, sailing away upon a great ship into the unknown? Did he see his glory days flying away upon angels' wings? I know what I saw in that dark moment. I saw . . .

Woe. Woe. Woe. What could be done by the mysterious, daring Matron O'Goole (that's me, remember)? What could be done for such a patient as this? With heavy heart, I did apply a dash of oils and wax to his blade and hilt. And I did wrap him in a veil of cloth. Twas as though Dave were a ghost or a mummified memory of a sword. Fie fie fie!

Ooooo! Ohhhh! As the fog closed in upon the castle, this matron knew that this patient, this sword, this noble David, could be treated and cured by but one person, and one person alone.

Recommendations:

Please send David to his creator, Mysto the dwarf. Only the most famous wizentor of them all can save Dave now.

Ooooooo! Ooohhhhh! What will become

of poor Dave? Woe!

Matron O'Goole liked reading
gothic stories. Can you tell? At
the moment, she's re-reading her
favourite, *Dr Chompenstein and the
Hospital of Horrors.*

CHAPTER 9

Knight Sir Louis did not hesitate. He found the castle dragon, Mac n Cheese, snoozing in the courtyard. He asked them if they would take Dave to Mysto. Concerned for the poor sword, Mac n Cheese flew off straight away with Dave.

Louis watched as Mac n Cheese flew away at top speed. Soon they had disappeared behind a cloud.

Mysto was on holiday, far to the south in the sunny Budgie Islands, but Louis was sure he wouldn't mind the interruption. Dave was Mysto's pride and joy, his finest invention.

But Louis felt strange without Dave at his side. What would he do if there was another emergency while Dave was away? He would need a temporary replacement. He needed a new, magic sword!

Louis went to see Pearlin in her laboratory and explained.

'But where am I going to get a magic sword?' he asked. 'It's not like they grow on trees.'

'Funny you should say that,' said Pearlin, 'cos I've been trying to make a bush that grows swords instead of thorns.'

'Sounds ideal!' said Louis.

'Would be,' said Pearlin, 'if it worked. All I get is tiny little shields that taste like barbecue sauce. Maybe I should ask Catalogue about it. She's the expert in plants and stuff.'

'Could you make a sword in the old-fashioned wizardy way?' asked Louis hopefully.

'Suppose,' said Pearlin. 'Not done it before. Would be interesting.'

But just at that moment, King Burt the Not Bad slammed open the door to the lab and strode in. He had a manic look about him.

'Louis! Pearlin! There you are. I need a fun park. And I need it NOW!'

'I'm sorry, your majesty, but I have

to find a new sword first,' explained Louis, 'in case the castle needs defending.'

'Excuses, excuses!' complained the king. 'I want an adventure park and I demand that we begin today. TODAY! Pearlin, you are the master of invention. This is your time to shine.'

Pearlin was rather excited by the idea. An adventure park powered by magic! Filled with fun inventions. Plus, the king was the king, and you sort of had to do what he asked.

'Sounds fun, your maj,' said Pearlin. 'Let's do it!' She turned to Louis apologetically. 'Sorry, Louis,' she said, 'I don't think I'm going to have time to make you a sweet new sword.'

'I understand,' said Louis sadly.

'But maybe you can get one here,' said Pearlin, and she handed over a piece of parchment. It was a flyer for a new market stall.

'Been hearing about it from all my other wizard and witch chums.'

Da Spell's

Market of the Magical

Whatever your magical needs, we're here.
Shop in store or order on magic parchment for
delivery by flying gargoyle.

Do you have a curse that needs lifting?
An ache that needs treating?
A toad that needs turning back into a prince?

We have . . .

Cures, Cloaks, Crystals, Candles
Potions, Powders, Pixie Promises
Spells, Stones, Sorcery, Swords

Not just your average witch service.
Our resident witch is always inventing!

Need a magical solution TODAY?
Then visit Da Spell's
For all your magical needs.

Find us at Hogford Market
The Kingdom of Squirrel Helm

CHAPTER 10

Louis strode to the castle stables where Clunkalot was recharging and composing poetry. Clunkie had been thinking about their underground adventure with diamonds. He printed out his latest haiku for Louis.

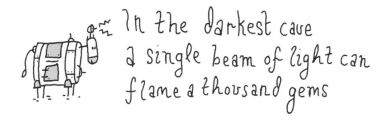

In the darkest cave
a single beam of light can
flame a thousand gems

'That's a good one, Clunkie,' said Louis. 'Now, let's get to Hogford. We've some shopping to do.'

Clunkalot circled over the great and ancient city of Hogford. It was a busy town, famous for its university, its libraries and its museums. It also had some great shops! Plus, it was where Louis' best friend Henrietta Catalogue lived. He planned to see her later, but first he wanted to get a new sword at Da Spell's.

They landed outside the market square. Louis wandered in amongst the many stalls. The market was impressive. You could buy anything you wanted. Food, clothes, soaps, toys, jewellery, and for some reason, horrible sculptures made of screws and wire. Clunkalot was particularly interested in one that looked like a tiny metal horse.

Louis walked around until he spied Da Spell's. It was a double length stall and was filled with all kinds of magical products.

The stall was manned by a very busy looking gnome.

Meanwhile, Cilla Da Spell was sitting at the back of the stall, magicking up new products as fast as she could. She was non-stop spellcasting! She was bursting with ideas. Becoming a full witch had been like pulling the cork from the bottle of her imagination.

To Do. LIST.
THINGS TO CONJURE

Crystal Ball Tea
Predict the future blend

Spider Web Berets
Nice and sticky.
won't fly away, even in a hurricane

Da Spell's own Slime Glow
Gloopy cream to make you
glow in the dark - literally.

She couldn't believe how well it was going. After having her idea to open a shop, she'd set up a stall in Hogford Market. Nobody else sold magical products. People were excited to see what she had on offer. On the first day, her products sold in a flash! On the second day, she set up a larger stall. People couldn't get enough of her magical provisions. She hoped that very soon she'd be able to move into a proper shop building. Before long, everyone would know the name Da Spell's! Her only problem was that the products sold out faster than she could make them.

It was while she was pondering this that she heard her sales gnome saying, 'Oh! Knight Sir Louis, champion knight and Deputy King of Castle Sideways, hero of the Kingdom of Squirrel Helm! At our stall! What a pleasure to meet you! I think you know my uncle, General Gnomus.'

Cilla immediately jumped up and ran to the front of the stall. Knight Sir Louis! Here? Where was he? Ah yes! There he was. Over by the magic swords!

CHAPTER 11

Louis checked out the magic swords at Da Spell's market stall.

The Jef Blade-zos
The El'lon Musketeer
The Steve Jabs

'Good morrow! What dost thou seek? How can I be of service to thee?' Cilla Da Spell stepped up beside the swords, smiling broadly. 'For I be Cilla, and this be my stall.'

'Oh, amazing,' said Louis. 'And yes, I'd love some help. My sword's not very well, so I need a replacement. Are these magic swords?'

'Tis true,' said Cilla. 'The Blade-zos be the least costly. It be middling good, and if it doth break, I canst magic another right soon. It be a simple enough spell.'

'Doesn't sound very strong,' said Louis.

'The Musketeer be a mighty sword,' said Cilla, 'though it canst be a little peevish. Unwatched, it may go a-wandering and chop things that it liketh not.'

'Not what I'm looking for,' said Louis anxiously.

'Then, perhaps you may prefer the Steve Jabs,' said Cilla, taking it down. 'It tooketh the longest to conjure. Dependable, looks handsome, though it is the most costly.'

Louis held the sword. It felt pretty good.

'It also hath extra features and is bound in excellent packaging,' said Cilla, and she flicked a switch on the side.

Steve started talking, slowly and smoothly. 'Hi. I'm Steve Jabs and I'm your magic sword for every occasion. I can play mood music, take great photos, and even provide directions to your next battle.'

Louis was impressed.

'Wow. I'll take Steve,' he said.

He paid Cilla and left the shop. It was time to find his friend Catalogue.

After he'd gone, Cilla had an idea. She stayed up all night, chanting the Steve Jabs spell over and over again. The next day she put up a poster at the stall.

The new Steve swords all sold within the hour. Time to make more!

CHAPTER 12

And now let's meet Catalogue the boar.

CATALOGUE

USED TO BE A NORMAL, SNUFFLING BOAR. WIZARD BAZOOKA HARRY GAVE HER A BIG BRAIN. AFTER THAT SHE STARTED WALKING AROUND ON HER HIND LEGS AND WEARING AN ELEGANT RUFF. SHE IS INTERESTED IN ADVENTURES, WEIRD PLANTS AND MAKING FRIENDS.

Catalogue has started to keep a personal diary. Here are some recent entries . . .

The Month ov Some-thing orrrr Other

Day the Second

Ho there, diar-ee. Ho there, me-self. Today iz another day. But with bells on. Cos today a lot of stuff haz changed for me. When I woz just a wild piggy boar, I didn't hav no name. I just called me-self oink and snnnnoorrrk. And all me friends woz called oink and snnnnoorrrk. And that woz that. But then I got given a big ~~brane~~ brain by a silly old wizard and then I was Mister Catalogue. Which was silly-as-a-sausage cos I is a lady. Anyways, then I was sometimes . . .

- Reader Catalogue
- (No name) Mildred Catalogue
- Henrietta Catalogue
- Magic Catalogue

But today I is getting a shy-nee new title.

Constable Catalogue

That's rite. I hav become a police piggy-wig. I fancied a new challenge after reading an amazing book. It was about a detective called Sherlock Hooves.

Sometimes rude peepul is calling the police 'the pigz'. Now they will be saying the

~~trooth~~ truth. (Although, I is not a regular-lar-lar piggy. I is a wild boar. Fact-o.)

Day the Fifth

I hav been a police wotsit for four days now and hav solved ~~fifteen~~ crimes already. Turns out having a sniffy-snooter like my nose is well-useful for snorting out criminals and their stolen doodars. I haz already been ~~promoated promooted~~ promoted. That means I is moving up in the world. I is now:

Sergeant Catalogue

Day the Twentieth

My job as a police ~~ossifer~~ officer is still going well and dandy. I have solved another seventy-two crimes on me own. The police co-mish-on-er (that's the boss) says I'm a starry star. She has promoted me again. I is now:

Inspector Catalogue

But I has a real tuff and hard case to solve. There's a big old ~~theeeef~~ thief in town and it don't smell like no person nor a ~~hanimal~~ animal. If anything, it leaves behind a sort of metal smell. Wot could it be? A robot? A giant evil walking talking spatula for flipping eggs? Who knows? Not me. But I is doing me best to find out.

P.S. I is looking forward to seeing me old chum Knight Sir Louis who is coming to Hogford.

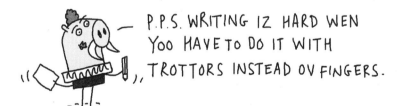 — P.P.S. WRITING IZ HARD WEN YOO HAVE TO DO IT WITH TROTTORS INSTEAD OV FINGERS.

CHAPTER 13

In this chapter, we're taking a quick breather. Let's catch up with Dave the Sword. He's strapped to the back of double-headed dragon Mac n Cheese.

Dave thinks . . . *It feels good up here in the clouds. Pretty clouds. Beautiful blue sky. Ahhh. Nice.*

Dave thinks . . . *It should be cold up here, but Mac n Cheese are lovely and warm. That will be the dragon fire in their belly keeping us toasty. Ahhh. Nice.*

Dave thinks . . . *It's nice to feel the breeze on my blade. Perhaps one day I'll sing again. Perhaps one day I'll be well enough. Oh, if I am, I'll do a really big concert. The walruses will love it!*

This wasn't as strange as it sounds, for when the wind blew across Dave's blade, he would sing. It sounded awful. It sounded so bad your ears would try to fold themselves closed. Only walruses enjoyed it. They would come from miles around to listen to Dave's wailing tunes.

Only last month, Louis had been in a fight with a giant evil sheep (Raymond the Rampaging Ram) out in a terrible storm. When Louis had lifted Dave into the storm winds, Dave had sung high and loud. The sound was so peculiar and disgusting that Raymond's woolly fleece had jumped off his body and run away all on its own.

And of course, during the battle, Dave's music had attracted a huge huddle of walruses.

While Dave remembered his glory days, Mac n Cheese flew onwards, over the sea and south to the sunny Budgie Islands.

CHAPTER 14

Meanwhile, back at Castle Sideways, plans for King Burt's adventure park were well underway.

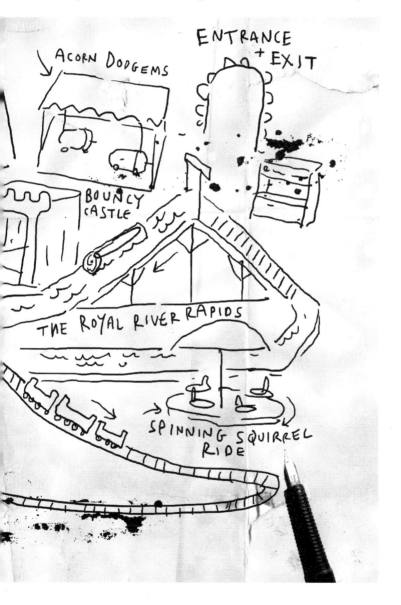

CHAPTER 15

Knight Sir Louis went to visit his old friend Catalogue. She had a shiny new office in Hogford Police Station. Louis' horse Clunkie waited outside, examining the serious looking police horses.

'I thought you were interested in plants,' said Louis while admiring Catalogue's shiny new inspector badge.

'Well, I still loves a strange mushroom or an unexpected dandelion,' said Catalogue. 'And it turns out a lot of clues has something to do with pesky plants what is poisonous, and stuff like pollen. That can show when a person was sneaking about somewhere, even when they says they wasn't.'

'Anything I can help with?' asked Louis.

'Yesses,' said Catalogue, 'cos I have a right tricky case and I needs your help.'

Catalogue pulled down a big chart showing a list of thefts around Hogford. In each case, gems or gold had gone missing. And in each case, someone nearby heard a strange whispering.

'The funny thing about these whispers, right,' explained Catalogue, 'is they appears in your head without going through your ears. That's a weird old whisper.'

'Something magical then,' said Louis.

'We needs to catch whoever it is red-handed. So, we needs to work out where they is going shopping next on their robbery tour.'

Louis joined the dots between the sites of the crimes. It was clear that whoever it was had started on the outskirts of Hogford and had been making

Hogford ~ Crime scenes

their way in circles, closer and closer to the centre of town.

'Looks like their next target is going to be right in the middle of Hogford. Here!'

Louis pointed to a building on the map.

'Of courses, horses,' said Catalogue, 'the Big Bank! Let's get down there pronto and wait for the cheeky burglar to fall into my trapping trotters.'

CHAPTER 16

It was a dark night. The moon was out, but its light was very dim (it was on a low-power setting to save energy). The Big Bank loomed over Hogford Main Square like a large building made of bricks.

There was hardly anyone or anything about. People were avoiding the square without really knowing why. When they came close, they would feel the hairs on their neck prickle. They would feel a flutter in their tummy. They would look over their shoulder with the strangest feeling that somebody was watching them from the shadows. It was all very spooky. And so, they would find a different way to wherever they were going. And if they were foolish enough to walk into the square, then they would feel their teeth suddenly chattering and they'd hear a strange whisper. It seemed to say . . .

Don't come near the Big Bank tonight. Oh no. Ha, ha, ho! No. Or you'll stub your toe. Or your nose will fall off. Or you'll turn into a really knobbly frog. Oh yes. Ha, ha, ho!

Louis, Clunkie and Catalogue were lying in wait inside the bank. They had let the bank manager,

Lord Pockets, know about their suspicions and he'd allowed them to hide inside.

Louis and Catalogue heard the staff leave and the bank manager lock up. They'd seen the light fade from the windows and heard the hoot of owls as night fell. And now they could both feel the strange spooky feelings. They could hear the whisper too. But they were prepared. Louis liked to carry a flask of Bravelington's Broth.

Bravelington's Broth

Original recipe by Wizard Gordon Fossil-Beard

Feeling afraid due to a nasty spell?

Getting the collywobbles thanks to a curse?

This magical soup can be taken in small spoonfuls.

Contains micro-gargoyles that bash and bish up horrible little whispers.

Brewed in Bravelington in small batches.

Approved by top wizentor Mysto.

Also available: Grumpy Gammon. Do you struggle in arguments? Try our new Grumpy Gammon. After you've eaten a slice, you'll disagree with everything like an expert. You won't even care if you're wrong, you'll just keep on arguing!

Louis and Catalogue took a spoonful each and soon felt the hot mixture burning away their spooky worries. Clunkalot's onboard computer had also picked up some strange airwaves. He'd put them through his decoder and it had written a poem. It went:

Ha Ha Ho Ha Ho
Ha Ha Ho Ha Ho Ho Ha
Ha Ha Oh Ha Ho

Clunkie didn't rate it very highly. Though it did make him feel very uneasy.

Louis, Catalogue and Clunkie hid behind the large main counter inside the bank and waited. Eventually Louis heard something. Something that wasn't a weird whisper.

'What's that scratching?' whispered Louis.

'Could be me,' said Catalogue. 'One of my constables is a flea and I get really itchy when he's around.'

'No, listen,' said Louis, putting his ear to the stone flagstone beneath his feet. 'It's coming from underneath us.'

Catalogue did the same and sure enough, she could hear something. A scratching. A whirring. A digging! And the noise was growing louder!

Before they had a chance to jump out of the way . . .

BOOM!

The floor exploded.

And leaping out in a splatter of mud and stones

BOOM!

was a cauldron. It jumped up and landed hard on the floor with a CLANG! Inside it, they could clearly see coins and gems sparkling.

'A cauldron?' said Catalogue, amazed.

'Looks like it,' said Louis. 'Maybe it belongs to a naughty witch or a nasty wizard!'

The cauldron didn't seem to notice Louis or Catalogue. It tottered on stiff metal legs towards the vaults. The vaults contained all the gold, gems, silver and other valuables belonging to the people of Hogford.

'Stop there!' announced Louis. 'In the name of the law!'

'That's right,' agreed Catalogue, 'you is under arrest. Though I've no idea where I'm going to put the handcuffs.'

The cauldron stopped and turned slowly. It obviously had a front and a back, though you wouldn't know from looking at it. It tipped slightly, one side to the other, like a wolf carefully examining its dinner before munching it down.

Then it charged.

Louis reached for his sword and leapt into action. And that's where things started to go wrong. Because Louis was used to Dave the sword. Dave was brave and tough and determined. Steve, on the other hand, was a different sort of sword.

'Hey there. I see you activated me. How can I help right now?' said Steve.

'We're in a fight for our lives!' said Louis urgently.

'That's great,' said Steve with an easy smile. 'So, first off, I'd like to recommend we warm-up.'

'We don't have time for a warm-up!' said Louis. 'The cauldron is coming! LOOK!'

Steve looked.

'OK. How would you like me to help? I can take photographs. A video. A slow-mo video? I can phone your mother, Champion Trixie, to ask for guidance. Or I could recommend a tasty meal to prepare before your fight begins.'

'NO!' shouted Louis. 'I NEED YOU TO FIGHT! NOW!'

'Fight a cauldron?' said Steve. 'Me? I'm sorry. I don't have any information on how to fight a

69

magic cauldron. But I can run away and find the answer. Have a nice day.'

And with that, Steve leapt from Louis' hand and dived towards a window. He smashed through and outside.

'ARGHHHHH!' said Louis as the cauldron bowled towards him.

SMASH!

I DON'T BELIEVE IT! THIS STEVE SWORD IS USELESS.

I'M TAKING MINE BACK TO THE SHOP.

AND ME.

ARE YOU LOOKING TO RETURN AN ITEM?

I CAN HELP YOU WITH THAT.

CHAPTER 17

The Cauldron of Chaos ran headlong towards Knight Sir Louis. Louis leapt behind one of the tall stone pillars. The cauldron made to follow but crashed straight into the pillar, which began to crumble. Then part of the roof gave way.

'Uh-oh!' said Catalogue. 'I think it's about to start raining stones!'

Sure enough, chunks of masonry fell from far above. This seemed to give the nasty cauldron an idea. Quickly it ran between the other stone pillars, bashing and boshing them hard. Soon all the pillars were crumbling.

Louis and Catalogue made a leap for Clunkalot.

'Fly, Clunkie!' said Louis and the robot horse

launched himself through the window that Steve the sword had already smashed.

Behind them, the cauldron turned and trotted back to the vaults, unconcerned by the collapsing bank. It smashed into the vaults, spilling out all the precious gold, silver, gems and antiques. It scooped up all the riches into its cauldron bowl on top of all the other stolen loot, then ran full pelt at a wall. It smashed its way out of the bank before the building finally came tumbling down. In all the chaos, Louis and Catalogue failed to see the cauldron making its escape.

When the dust settled over Hogford Main Square, Louis looked over the rubble and said, 'Well. That plan didn't go to plan.'

Meanwhile the cauldron found its way to a back alley. It staggered under the weight of its stolen goods.

It thought to itself, *Finally! I'm full to the brim. It's time! Ha, ha, ho!*

And then the cauldron started to spin, and glow a strange orange colour, almost like it was some giant, horrible pumpkin. And then the gold and silver and gems inside it started to melt into a giant magical soup. And then there was the sound of gurgling and the soup started to vanish as though it was being sucked down a plug hole in a bath. In fact, it was being turned into magical power! At last, the cauldron stopped spinning and the glow vanished.

There was nothing left inside the cauldron. But the cauldron itself was transformed. It was no longer cracked, or dull or dented. It was shiny and as orange as a pumpkin! It looked brand new. And then it did something it hadn't done for a long, loong, looooong time. It leapt into the air . . . and flew!

CHAPTER 18

And now a quick review of all the faces Lord Pockets made after he discovered his bank had been emptied of all its treasures and destroyed:

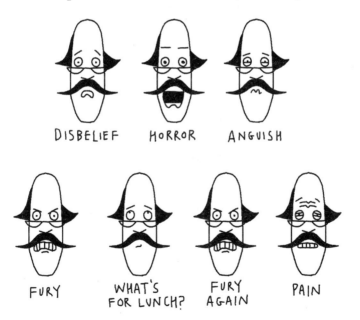

DISBELIEF   HORROR   ANGUISH

FURY   WHAT'S FOR LUNCH?   FURY AGAIN   PAIN

SADNESS

MORE
FURY

WORRY

CALLING THE
CUSTOMERS

DETERMINATION

CALLING THE
BUILDERS

CUP OF TEA.
DA SPELL'S CALMING
CHAMOMILE BLEND

CHAPTER 19

And now over to the DARK AGES NEWS TEAM with Lady Shufflepaper and Squire Chattymouth.

NEWS FLASH! DUM BONG DUM BONG BING-A LING-A LING

SC: Hello and welcome to the news. Reports have been coming in from across the Many Kingdoms of a shiny, orange, flying cauldron.

LS: The cauldron, dubbed the Cauldron of Chaos, has been greedily scooping up any riches it can find.

SC: So far, it's emptied the Bank of Brrrrrland, the Vaults of Verdig and the Treasury of Tumblin' Klatterbang.

LS: The Republic of Klaptrap and their neighbour Proud Fidget have also had their savings raided. The Principality of Plopp has yet to be attacked.

SC: Over now to our Magic Correspondent, Daniel Wigglewand. Daniel, you're in Plopp . . . what's the situation?

DW: Well, Gerald, I can tell you people here are worried. It seems likely that Plopp will be the next victim of the dreaded cauldron. Princess Penny, Paymaster of the Principality of Plopp, has told me that she is perturbed, pensive and preoccupied about the problem.

SC: I'm sure she is, Daniel. And after this I will be looking in my dictionary to work out what all those words mean.

DW: And oh! WAIT! There's something happening here. Right now! LIVE! Yes. I can see it flying in. An orange, shiny cauldron. It's broken through the clouds above and is heading right for the Royal Mint!

LS: Mint? Is the cauldron interested in refreshing herbs too?

DW: No, mint as in the place where they make money!

SC: Oh, yes. Mint. We knew that. Honest.

DW: And yes, it's going straight in and gobbling up the coins. This is—

LS: And, oh dear, it looks like we've lost our magical connection to Daniel. But it sounds like the Principality of Plopp is

about to see its luck plunge and plummet and
 its money perish permanently.

SC: OK, I really need that dictionary now.

END OF
NEWS
FLASH!

BING·A
LING·A
LING
DUM BONG
DUM BONG

CHAPTER

DICTIONARY

And now Argie the librarian reads from the Official Hogford Illustrated Dictionary.

Pensive

thoughtful but sad

Perish

to die

Permanent

lasting for ever

Perturb

to upset, to trouble someone's thoughts

Plummet

to fall quickly

Plunge

to dive or fall into water

Preoccupy

to think about something so much, there's no room to think about other things

Oh, and also:

Mint

a place where money is made!

CHAPTER 20

Louis had been following the news. It was clear that the Many Kingdoms were up against a new kind of baddy. Louis had fought nothing like it before. He'd fought evil wizards, potatoes, dragons, gnomes, slime monsters and a giant snowball. Defeating this cauldron would require a new strategy. He needed expert advice. But from whom?

'Let's check in the librararararararar— place where the books are,' said Catalogue.

And so, they went to the library. Catalogue's friend Argie the cyclops was a librarian and helped them hunt through the archives. While Louis was looking for something, anything that might help, he saw a familiar face.

Steve Jabs.

Steve was sitting at one of the library tables next to a stack of books. He was muttering to himself as he read.

'Sel-pum-a-wel-tu-nu-rish-pel-a-so.'

Steve was reading books at top speed.

'Hey there, Sir Louis, I'm doing just as I promised and looking for an answer to your question.'

'Which question?' said Louis. A couple of days had already passed since his battle at the bank in Hogford.

'You know,' said Steve, 'how to defeat a magic cauldron.'

'Oh, yes,' said Louis. 'I thought you were just afraid and had decided to run away.'

'Well, it was very frightening,' explained Steve, 'because I had no idea what to do. Sadly, there doesn't seem to be anything useful in the history books about a magic cauldron. But I did find a children's fairy story. Maybe that could be useful?'

Louis and Catalogue sat down to read the book. It was large and square with lots of pictures. It was old. Very old. The spine was weak. The paper like tissue. The pictures were old-fashioned and the colour had faded from the pages. Louis turned the first page.

CHAPTER
FAIRY STORY

THE TALE OF THE GREEDY CAULDRON

BY THE BROTHERS GRIMM-A-LING-A-DING-DONG

Once upon a time, in a land far away, there was a wizard called Florin.

Florin liked to help his fellow villagers.

He would make them potions. They would pay with a silver coin.

Florin loved magic. But more than magic, he loved money.

He decided to make himself a very special cauldron.

He made it strong, with four short legs, and painted it bright orange, his favourite colour.

When it was finished, Florin cast three spells on the cauldron.

The first spell made it fly.

The second spell made it think.

And the third spell gave the cauldron an appetite.

But it wasn't an appetite for food. It was an appetite for riches!

Florin sent the cauldron off to find treasure.

Florin congratulated himself: 'I'm such a clever wizard! Soon I'll be the richest person in the land.'

But things quickly went wrong. The cauldron didn't care where it found riches. It didn't look for lost pennies. It didn't search for gems in caves. That would take too long! So instead, the cauldron stole all it could.

Worse still, because it was even greedier than Florin, it decided to keep it all for itself!

Florin didn't see a penny.

When the people of the village and the land around discovered who had made the cauldron, they were not happy.

'What are you going to do to make things right?' demanded the people.

Florin didn't know what to do.

He felt like a fool.

He felt scared.

And because he felt scared and foolish, his magic left him.

Florin ran away.

Eventually he found a high hill, so bleak and cold that no one else lived there.

'I'll stay here for ever,' he said to himself. 'They won't find me here.'

He was right, too. A year and a day later, Florin was still alone. He had not seen a single person.

'What use are riches if you don't have friends?' he said to himself.

He remembered how the villagers used to smile and wave at him.

The memory was sweet.

He remembered how his magic used to make their lives better.

That memory was sweeter still.

He remembered how it was to be a valued member of the village.

And then he felt a tingle at the end of his nose.

And a tingle in his finger.

And a little in his toes.

Magic.

He felt some magic return.

If I'm ever to go home, he thought to himself, *I must stop the cauldron and I must give everything back that it has stolen.*

During his time on the hill, Florin had made himself a little garden for growing vegetables.

He looked over and saw that a bunch of celery was almost ready.

He cast a spell and the stalks turned golden!

Surely, if the cauldron saw the stalks, it would mistake them for real gold.

It would stop here and steal the celery.

Then Florin finished his spell by saying, 'Whoever eats this celery must undo all they have done!'

Florin sat and waited.

He watched the skies.

He waited for another year and a day.

Then at last, the cauldron appeared in the

sky. It was flying across the land, looking for more riches to steal.

When it flew over the hill, sure enough, it spied the golden celery.

It dived down and scooped up the vegetables in one great gulp.

Yes, the cauldron swallowed the celery and the spell began its task.

And oh, what a sight! The cauldron shivered and shuddered and spun about.

Then off it flew to give back all that it had taken.

Florin danced for joy. His plan had worked.

The cauldron did not want to give up its riches, but the magic made it return every coin, every gem and every jewel it had stolen.

Florin returned home, and he was welcomed once more.

He promised his friends never to be greedy again.

CHAPTER

VEGETABLES

Louis and Catalogue finished reading the fairy story.

'Are you thinking it's an actual, real story?' wondered Catalogue.

'Maybe some of it's true,' said Louis.

Louis flicked through the fairy story again. Perhaps once upon a time this had happened? Perhaps it had become a rumour, and then a myth, and then a fairy story? It wasn't much to go on, but the cauldron in the tale really did sound like the one they'd just met. Perhaps the cure for their problems was here in this little picture book? It was all he had to go on.

'There's no mention that the cauldron was

destroyed,' said Louis, thinking aloud. 'That bit about the celery was interesting.'

'I thunk that too,' said Catalogue. 'Veggies is always turning up in our quests.'

This was a fact. They had met evil potatoes, a giant parsnip, an ice cucumber, ripe yellow corn on the cobs for a magic potion and even a carrot who'd become Prime Minister.

'But where do you find magic celery?' he wondered aloud.

Steve Jabs knew the answer. He'd already read most of the books in the travel section.

'We need to go to Transylwoofia,' he piped up, pointing his blade at a chunky, black and orange book.

CHAPTER 21

Hello. We all know something about the country of Transylwoofia. You may have read the stories about Count Woofula. Or perhaps have watched the play about Frankenbark. You may even have enjoyed the spooky stories of the Three Billy Ghosts Gruff. But I have been to Transylwoofia to discover the reality.

On my visit to Transylwoofia, I found some of the most wonderful animals and plants. There are the purring pumpkins, a sort of a cross between a cat and a squash. There are the strawberry spiders who weave the tastiest, fruitiest webs.

And then, there is the Celery of Shocks.

This vegetable grows only on one bleak hill in Transylwoofia. Almost nothing else grows there. The winds are cold and strong all year round. But this is where the celery thrives. This rare variety of celery spends most of its life underground, avoiding the foul winds, but from time to time it thrusts itself out of the soil and into the light of the sun. When it does this, the celery squeaks loudly, making a noise that shocks anyone walking by. And that is, no doubt, where the name comes from.

The celery can be pressed to make a strong, healthy drink. It is said that the juice can suck the naughtiness out of anything and anyone. Because of this power, the celery became very desirable. More and more people came to pick it until it was almost wiped out for ever. To protect this special plant, a band of warrior monks lives on the bleak hill.

They defend the celery from anyone who would pick it. They are the legendary Were-Whoodles.

Part Poodle. Part Wheaten Terrier.
Part Werewolf.

Sadly, the Were-Whoodles are so protective that nobody has been able to get near the Celery of Shocks for many, many years.

Louis closed the book and looked at his friend, Catalogue.

'This celery sounds perfect! How do you fancy a trip to Transylwoofia?'

'I'm in,' said Catalogue. 'First of all, I is always interested in funny plants what do interesting thingies. And second, I have to find out if there's such a thing as a Were-Whoodle.'

'There's no time to waste,' said Louis. 'Next time we face that cauldron, I want to be ready with a celery smoothie.'

'What about you, Steve?' asked Catalogue. 'Is you coming along or staying to read the whole librarararar— all the books?'

'I think I'm ready for a new adventure,' said Steve.

A moment later, they were waving goodbye to Hogford. They climbed onto Clunkalot and launched into the air. Clunkie wrote a poem to celebrate their new quest.

To Transylwoofia
Where Were-Whoodles watch wary
of naughty nibblers.

CHAPTER 22

Meanwhile, back at Castle Sideways, the construction of the fun park was in full flow. Pearlin was having a whale of a time. The park was the biggest, best thing she'd invented yet.

Everything was themed around the king and the castle. Under construction was:

- Train of princely carriages
- Acorn-shaped dodgems
- The Royal River Rapids
- A unicorn carousel
- Wizardy waltzers
- The Throne Rollercoaster
- Spinning squirrel ride
- Bouncy castle
- Food stalls
- Entrance and exit barrier.

The whole thing was powered with magic. Pearlin had set up a special crystal ball. The magical power inside it was concentrated fun and giggles magic.

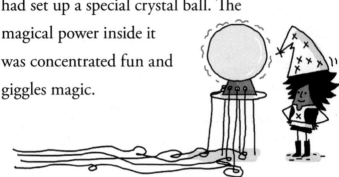

'I reckon this'll keep the park running for a whole season,' she said.

King Burt was thrilled and very, very excited.

'Oh, this really is the best idea I ever stole from somebody else. The best thing that's ever happened! Yahoo! When does it open? When? When?'

Pearlin looked around at the construction.

'Another two or three days, I reckon,' she said. 'Then we open to the world. It's gonna be magic! But . . . we still don't have a good name for it.'

'I've been thinking about that,' said the king. 'And I've decided on Squirrel Helm's Really

Imperial Merry Playground of Sunny Awesome Nice Delightful Wonderful Incredible Cheery Hurrahs!'

'Bit long, ain't it?' questioned Pearlin. 'Plus, the first letters spell out SHRIMP SANDWICH.'

'Oh, bother,' said Burt, deflated.

'Maybe just call it the Squirrel Helm Realm of Wonder?"

'No. Wait! I've got a better idea,' said King Burt. 'Let's call it . . . the Squirrel Helm Realm of Wonder!'

THAT'S WHAT PEARLIN JUST SAID!

YEAH, BUT YOU KNOW WHAT THE KING'S LIKE!

'Yeah, right,' said Pearlin, who also knew what the king was like. 'Great idea, your majestic whatever. Now, back to work I go, or I'll never get it finished.'

King Burt ordered his throne to be brought outside so he could sit and watch as the theme park was completed, piece by piece.

CHAPTER 23

Cilla's shop was doing splendidly. She was now well-known around Hogford. People recognised that she wasn't some ordinary witch. She didn't hide out in the deep, dark woods. She didn't keep a soggy toad or a scary cat or even a staring owl. She was making people rethink what a witch could be. For a start she had potions that no other witch sold. She was an innovator! She was doing and making things no witch had done before.

But this still wasn't enough for Cilla. She wanted to be known for her amazing skills beyond Hogford. She wanted to be appreciated by people throughout the whole kingdom. And beyond that too! She imagined going on a world tour one day, visiting the Many Kingdoms, greeting her many fans.

The problem was, Cilla was running out of new ideas. She had worked so hard and invented so many ace new powders, spells, curses, potions, hexes and magical objects. Now it felt as though someone had emptied her brain of new ideas. Cilla was worried that without new products to sell, people would grow tired of her. Then instead of a world tour, it would be . . .

How could she come up with new ideas? What did she have to do?

A tiny voice inside her said, 'It wouldst be wondrous to have a good friend, no? Thence thou couldst craft new ideas with them. Why shouldst a person create alone?'

But a bigger voice inside her said, 'I needeth not friends. I needeth fans!'

The more she worried about running out of ideas, the worse it became. Eventually, Cilla couldn't think of anything new, at all. Oh well. She would just have to keep selling the same old stuff until she had a brainwave.

Luckily it wasn't all bad news. At least she hadn't put her money in the Hogford bank. She'd have lost it all. To begin with, Cilla had kept her money at home, inside her hut on duck legs. But she'd made so much money from her shop, that she'd had to put it somewhere else. Now she also had a giant moneybox on grasshopper legs. Every time it jumped, it jingled with coins. She was sure it was quite safe there.

CHAPTER 24

Now, I don't know about you, but I'm wondering how poor Dave is getting on.

Mac n Cheese arrived in the beautiful Budgie Islands and soon found the legendary wizentor Mysto. They handed over Dave, who was close to fading away for ever. It was all very dramatic, like one of those hospital dramas!

CHAPTER A

Now, let's rejoin Louis on his quest to Transylwoofia.

The Land of Transylwoofia lay south-east of Squirrel Helm. Few travellers made it from one country to the other. Why? The people of Squirrel Helm were convinced that the people of Transylwoofia were all bloodthirsty wolf creatures. Meanwhile, the people of Transylwoofia thought their neighbours must be ten-foot squirrels with pointy metal helmets.

There was another reason too – the famous River Sploosh – a huge raging river that marked the border between the two countries.

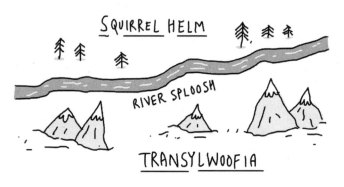

Nobody had yet built a bridge across the river. It was too wide. Too fast. And too full of sabre-toothed salmon. It wasn't the sort of place to go swimming. Not for very long anyway.

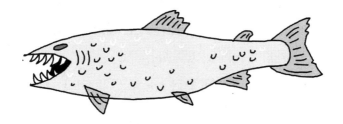

There were other ways to reach Transylwoofia. You could go the long way, assuming you survived the journey through deep, dark woods or through the dangerous deserts of Doooooom! The best way (of course) was to fly! But not many people had their very own robot horse.

Sir Louis watched the world flash by below. He marvelled at the huge river. He was excited to be travelling somewhere new again. He had only ever heard rumours, myths and legends about Transylwoofia. Now, he would get to see it with his own eyes.

They flew low over the river, listening to its impressive roar as it gushed onwards. They watched the salmon leap up and try to snap them. And then the river was behind them! Ahead were wide sweeping valleys with trees poking out of murky mists. Pointy castles sat on snow-capped mountains. Eventually night began to fall and bats started to flit up and around Clunkie and his passengers. The bats had never seen a flying horse before. They were really quite excited!

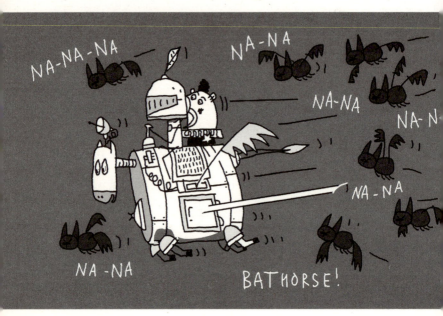

As the sun dipped below the horizon, turning blood-red for extra drama, the travellers started to think about resting for the night.

'It's almost my beddy-byes time,' said Catalogue, 'plus my bum-bottom has gone to sleep from all this sitting!'

'Yes, it's been a looooong journey,' agreed Louis. 'I think we might have to find a field or something. We can camp inside Clunkie's tummy.'

'Hang on a mo,' said Catalogue, and pointed a trotter. 'What's that twinkly twinkler over there?'

Sure enough, lights were coming on in a town on the horizon.

But then Louis noticed a hump of rocky hills ahead.

'And look over there,' said Louis. 'I bet there's a cave we could hide in.'

Time for you to help Louis and Catalogue:
If you think they should go to the town, then go to Chapter B.

If you think they should go to the rocky hills, then go to Chapter C.

If you think they should carry on flying until they find the Were-Whoodles, then go to Chapter E.

CHAPTER B

Clunkie turned towards the twinkling lights. The town, whose name was Angreemob, was surrounded by a high wall. The town gates were locked for the night, but that wasn't a problem for Clunkalot. He hovered over the town and very gently, very quietly, landed in a dark, deserted street. Yellow light streamed out from the windows of a nearby inn.

'Ooh! Maybe we can get a nice, cosy room in this place,' suggested Catalogue.

They looked up at the sign. The inn was called the Vicious Swan.

'Funny name,' said Catalogue. 'Though I have met a few swans like that.'

Louis and Catalogue walked into the Vicious Swan. It was packed with people. Almost immediately, everyone stopped talking and turned to look at the strangers.

Catalogue smiled through gritted teeth and told them all, 'Goodbye. We is just leaving.'

But a giant man, as tall as he was wide, had already barred the way out.

'Who are you?' barked the man who turned out to be the innkeeper.

'They're strangers!' shouted another.

'We don't like strangers,' said a third.

'Strangers are strange!' agreed a fourth.

Then the rest of the place joined in. They were all talking at once. It sounded like a massive argument. Except they weren't arguing. They were all agreeing. Louis and Catalogue were most definitely strangers. And they really didn't like strangers.

Louis looked for an escape route. But then another voice rang out. It was clear and commanding and everyone stopped to listen.

'They are with me. Da! Da! My friends. Over here!'

The voice came from a man sitting alone at one of the tables. He was wearing a cloak with the hood pulled over his head, so it was impossible to see what he looked like.

'Over here, friends. And innkeeper, bring them soup. And don't be taking lots of time. Da?'

The giant innkeeper eyed Catalogue and Louis with suspicion. Catalogue tried a smile and said, 'Ooh, yeah. Mushroomy soup if you got it.'

'You'll get what you're given,' said the innkeeper rudely.

Everyone went back to their own business. Louis and Catalogue walked to the table and sat down.

'Thank you for helping us,' said Louis. 'I'm Knight Sir Louis. This is Catalogue.'

'Da! Welcome, travellers. Your names are unusual. Do you come from distant lands? I would like to hear about them. And especially the food!'

The man pulled back his hood to reveal pointy ears, dark hair and a pair of rather obvious fangs.

'My name is Sir Petrify. I am . . . how do you say? Food critic! I rove and travel land looking for interesting dinners.'

'Excuse me for asking,' said Catalogue with a gulp, 'but I can't help noticing you is looking like a bloodsucking vampire.'

'Vampire, yes. You got me there. But bloodsucking. Not so much. The old vampires are obsessed with all that blood stuff. Being scary. Spooky. Whatever. Pah! It turns out there is only one thing in blood that we really need. Iron!'

'Iron? Like metal? You saying blood has got metal in it? You sure?' asked Catalogue.

'Oh, yes. And you can't argue with science,' said Sir Petrify. 'At least, that's what my friend Doctor Thinkinstein says.'

'So, what do you eat?' asked Louis, one hand ready on his sword.

YOU CAN'T ARGUE WITH SCIENCE

'I prefer chickpeas and a dried apricot. Lots of iron in those. Mm-mm!'

'Well, that's a mighty relief,' said Catalogue.

'Still, it comes in handy being a vampire sometimes,' said Sir Petrify. 'The people here know to leave me alone.'

He looked around at the people in the inn.

'I came here to try the food. But it is very bad. The people of Angreemob mostly stay within the walls of the town. They don't like visitors and they really don't like change.'

The innkeeper clattered down two bowls of soup for Louis and Catalogue. Catalogue looked at hers, sniffed and asked, 'Scuse me, can I have a shake of pepper in here?'

'No,' said the innkeeper and walked off.

'See,' said Sir Petrify. 'They won't even change the soup!'

'If you like to travel, then I wonder if you can help us,' said Louis. 'Do you know where we can find the Were-Whoodles and their Celery of Shocks?'

Once again, the whole inn went quiet. The people turned to look at Louis and Catalogue once more.

'Hey, vampire! Who are these strange strangers you're talking to? They ask strange questions!'

Sir Petrify held up his hands for calm and announced, 'Just a little joke amongst friends, that's all!'

And then he turned to Louis and Catalogue and whispered, 'I think we'd better leave soon before the crowd turns ugly. Well . . . uglier. But I can help you.'

Sir Petrify unfolded a map from somewhere inside his cloak and laid it on the table.

'This is my map of Transylwoofia. You may have this copy for a small price.'

'Name it,' said Louis, keen to get on his way. He saw that some of the crowd were gathering together, pointing at them and grinding their teeth. Were they hoping for a fight? Almost certainly.

'My price is a recipe,' said Sir Petrify. 'I would like to know what you are eating in your country.

What flavours you use. I would really like to try something new.'

Louis smiled. 'If you follow us outside, I'll ask my robot horse to print out an entire book of recipes!'

Sir Petrify smiled back. This really showed off his teeth. Catalogue decided that she preferred it when their new friend didn't smile. Catalogue and Louis swallowed down their hot soup. All three of them pretended they were off to the toilet.

'Oh, I really must go for a tinkle, da,' said Sir Petrify loud enough for the villagers to hear.

'Me too,' agreed Louis.

'Me three,' said Catalogue.

'And then we will definitely come back to our table,' fibbed Sir Petrify. 'Da, for sure!'

In the toilet, they climbed out the back window and then they ran around to the front and found Clunkalot.

'Do you want to leap on too?' Louis asked Sir Petrify.

'No need,' he said, and pointed to a dark alleyway. A huge hairy bat stepped out and opened its large leathery wings.

Catalogue almost fell off Clunkie in surprise.

'Meet my trusty bat, Dennis,' said Sir Petrify. 'He doesn't suck blood either, in case you are wondering. He only eats giant creepy-crawlies like grotipedes and mega-spiders.'

'Phew,' said Catalogue. 'That's a relief. Hang on. No, it isn't. Are you saying there is massive spiders here in Transylwoofia?'

'Oh yes,' confirmed Sir Petrify. 'We have five thousand different types of spider. Including the strawberry spider. Delicious! Though not much iron. It's more like a candy.'

'Right,' said Catalogue. 'I'm thinking we need to get this mission over as soon as poss!'

'Agreed,' said Louis, pointing to the Vicious Swan.

The doors cracked open. The mob spilt out, running towards them and shouting things like, 'There they are! Strange strangers being strange about strange things!'

Clunkalot leapt into the air and Dennis the Bat launched alongside him.

As they rose into the air, Sir Petrify said, 'You have the map, so now you can find the Were-Whoodles. But you won't get past them unless you have something silver!'

After handing over the book of recipes, they waved goodbye to Petrify and flew on into the night.

'On to the next chapter,' said Louis.

'Fine by me,' said Catalogue.

Louis noticed the hump of rocky hills ahead again. But then Catalogue spied something else. A giant castle, with huge pointy spires.

Time for you to help Louis and Catalogue:

If you think they should go to the castle, then go to Chapter D.

If you think they should go to the rocky hills, then go to Chapter C.

If you think they should carry on flying until they find the Were-Whoodles, then go to Chapter E.

CHAPTER C

Louis, Catalogue and Clunkalot raced on towards the rocky hills. It was as if a giant had dropped some enormous smooth stones from the sky. Clunkie circled around and landed amongst them. Perhaps they could find a cosy place to sleep?

Soon, they found a good-sized cave, away from the wind.

'This is a nice old spot,' said Catalogue. 'Surprising nobody's turned it into a secret little home.'

'I say,' said a voice right behind them, 'visitors! To this, my secret little home!'

They spun around to see a skeleton.

'Whoa! A talking skelling-ellington!' shouted

Catalogue in surprise. 'What are you? How are you? Who are you?'

'Nobody,' said the skeleton.

'Well, you must be somebody,' said Catalogue, 'cos I can see you with me own eyeballs.'

'I mean, my name is Nobody. Because I have . . . no body.'

'Fair enough,' said Catalogue.

'Good to meet you, Nobody,' said Louis bravely. 'We were just looking for somewhere to rest for the night. We didn't mean to trespass.'

'I really don't mind, you know. I haven't seen anyone for ages. I'm guessing you're strangers to these parts?'

'Yes,' said Louis. 'We are on a mission to get some celery from the Were-Whoodles.'

'Oh yes, of course,' said Nobody wistfully. 'Brave folks are always trying that.'

'And how does it usually end?' asked Catalogue.

'The brave folks get bitten, I'm afraid. And then

they also turn into Were-Whoodles. With every failed mission, there are more and more Were-Whoodles. Terrible business.'

'Well, there must be some way of getting that celery!' said Louis.

'Quite right,' said Nobody. 'And it's lucky you found me, because I have just what you need.'

Nobody clapped his hands and from deep inside the cave there came the gentle tapping of many, many feet. A little army of tiny, cute spiders emerged from the darkness.

'That's not creepy at all,' said Catalogue, lying through her teeth.

'Were-Whoodles fear only one thing,' explained Nobody. 'Silver! And these are silver spiders. They can spin you a suit or some pyjamas or even a onesie from their silver thread. The Were-Whoodles won't be able to get near you.'

'I'm guessing you're not going to give us this for free,' said Louis.

'There is a small price,' said Nobody.

'Probably want us to find you a body, don't you?' said Catalogue grimly.

'Sort of,' said Nobody. 'The spiders aren't much company. I wouldn't mind someone else to talk to. It's very lonely here.'

Louis and Catalogue paced around, trying to work out how to find a friend for Nobody. Maybe one of them would have to stay? But they couldn't stay for ever! Clunkalot was standing nearby, watching. He printed out a haiku poem.

Some problems are solved
By looking inside yourself.
Trash can be treasure.

Catalogue read it and shook her head. 'Reads more like a riddle than a poem.'

Louis read it a few times, then Clunkie gave an extra hint and opened up the hatch on the side of his body.

'Of course!' said Louis. 'Clunkie has loads of

spare parts. Maybe we can make Nobody a little robot friend?'

Neither Louis nor Catalogue were experts at inventions. That was Pearlin's talent. But with some help from Clunkalot, they managed to put together a small, shuffling robot. They used black and white paint to make it look like a little skeleton. Louis switched it on.

'Hello,' said the robot. 'What's my name?'

'Good question,' said Louis, turning to Nobody. 'What shall we call it?'

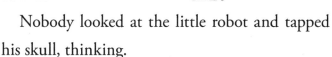

Nobody looked at the little robot and tapped his skull, thinking.

'I know,' said Nobody, 'your name is No-one!'

'Hello,' said the robot, happily. 'I am No-one!'

A short while later, the spiders had woven some silver onesies for Louis, Clunkalot and Catalogue. Perfect!

It was lovely to see Nobody with his new friend. But Louis and Catalogue were still very tired. It turned out skeletons and robots didn't ever go to bed. Their clattering and bleeping made it impossible to fall asleep. So, they decided to head off once again.

As they departed, they waved goodbye.

'Farewell, Nobody and goodbye, No-one.'

Louis could see the twinkling light of a town nearby.

And Catalogue saw the spires of a castle.

Time for you to help Louis and Catalogue:

If you think they should go to the castle, then go to Chapter D.

If you think they should go to the town, then go to Chapter B.

If you think they should carry on flying until they find the Were-Whoodles, then go to Chapter E.

CHAPTER

Louis, Catalogue and Clunkalot sailed through the sky towards the spookiest castle they'd ever seen. This was not an accident.

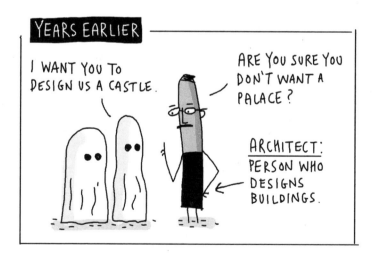

Castle Spooky-Woo looked about as much fun as a nettle salad. But it did at least have a roof and presumably some bedrooms and therefore beds to sleep in. When Louis knocked on the huge door, there was no answer, but the door did creak open very slowly on its own. After investigating a few dark passageways, they found a room with some large, cosy beds. Louis and Catalogue climbed in, hoping for a good night's sleep. Clunkalot stood nearby, powered down and went into standby mode.

Meanwhile, the inhabitants of the castle gathered in a dark corner.

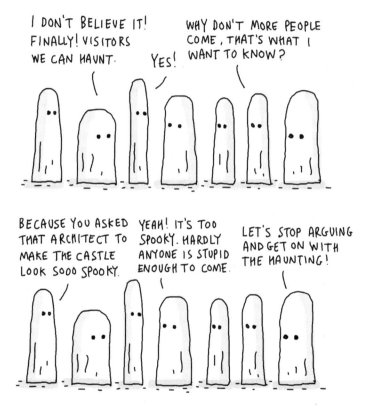

Louis and Catalogue were just about to fall asleep when they felt a cold breeze blowing. Then they heard several voices wailing. The ghosts floated into their room. They circled and wailed, hoping to frighten the visitors.

'Ooooooooooo!'

'Whooooaaaaa!'

Catalogue was a brave boar, but she was discovering that Transylwoofia was full of all the things she liked the least. Spooky things. She dived under the covers. But the ghosts continued.

'Oooooaaaaah!'

'Muuuurrrrrrr!'

It was quite an effective haunting until the smallest ghost quickly blurted out, 'Boo-boo-boo-boo-boo-boo!'

Catalogue poked her head out of the covers, chuckled and said, 'Eh? Boo-boo-boo-boo. Ha! You what? That's not scary.'

Another of the ghosts agreed. 'Exactly! If anything, it's silly.'

'It should be more like boooooooooooo,' said a third ghost.

'Let's just stop arguing and frighten them!' said a fourth.

Louis stepped out of bed and reached for his sword.

'Ghosts! Go! You don't frighten us,' shouted Louis.

He was thinking that his sword Dave would help frighten them away! But, of course, Dave wasn't there. It was Steve Jabs.

Steve looked at the floating spectres and said, 'Hey there. Looks like you're having a party! Would you like some hints and tips on how to have a great time?'

'This isn't a party!' said a ghost.

'We're not trying to give you a fun time!' said another.

'We are here to shock and stun!' said a third.

'I've seen scarier things in me own handkerchief,' said Catalogue. 'I'm no fan of spooky stuff. But you lot are not giving me shivers nor quivers nor nothing. Sorry.'

'Oh, what's the point?' said one ghost, giving up.

'Yeah,' said another. 'No one wants to come here. And when they do, we can't even frighten them.'

Meanwhile, Steve Jabs continued chatting. 'It looks like this is a party with a spooky theme. Try carving pumpkins. Make a cake in the shape of a spider. Dress up. Sing funny songs about monsters. I can make you a playlist!'

'You know,' said Louis, sympathising with the poor ghosts, 'I think Steve's idea is a good one. Lots of people like parties and dressing up in spooky stuff.'

'Yeah, right,' agreed Catalogue, 'you could make this into a fun castle with spooky parties. Bound to get more people coming then.'

A short while later, Steve Jabs had helped the ghosts plan a whole new spooky party business. They couldn't wait to get started.

'How can we repay you?' asked the ghosts.

'You don't have to,' said Louis. 'We only came to stay the night. We're on our way to get some celery from the Were-Whoodles.'

'Then we have the perfect gift,' said one ghost. It flew off and returned with a small bag, tied at the neck with rope.

'This bag contains a cold, spooky wind,'

explained the ghost. 'Once you have the celery, open the bag and let the wind out.'

'What for?' asked Catalogue.

'You'll see!' said the ghost.

Louis, Catalogue, Steve and Clunkalot headed off once more. They saw the twinkling town and the rocky hills nearby.

Time for you to help Louis and Catalogue:
If you think they should go to the town, go to Chapter B.

If you think they should go to the rocky hills, go to Chapter C.

If you think they should carry on flying until they find the Were-Whoodles, then go to Chapter E.

CHAPTER E

If you've read chapters B, C and D, then go to Chapter F!

If you've not read all three of B, C and D, then . . .

. . . oh! A great dark cloud gathers above Louis, Catalogue and Clunkalot and suddenly a bolt of lightning cracks down onto them! BOOM! A moment later they are magically transported. They find themselves back by the great River Sploosh in Chapter A!

SO, BASICALLY THAT IS A MASSIVE HINT THAT WE NEED TO READ ALL THOSE CHAPTERS BEFORE GETTING TO CHAPTER F?

I THINK SO.   HINT! HINT!

CHAPTER F

At last, Louis and Catalogue saw the great hill of the Were-Whoodles ahead of them. A huge full moon glistened over the top of the hill like a giant, shiny cannonball.

'What is a Whoodle, anyway?' asked Catalogue.

'Some sort of Poodle, I think,' said Louis.

'Crossed with a wh . . . wh . . . what? A whale?' wondered Catalogue.

'Crossed with a Wheaten Terrier,' explained

Steve Jabs who had read a book about dogs in the library and remembered every word.

Louis brought Clunkalot down in a clump of trees not far from the hill. He'd heard that were-creatures were stronger at night, especially during a full moon. He planned to reach the summit at midday. Surely, they would be weaker when the sun was high? At last, it was time to sleep.

ZZZZZZZZz

CHAPTER 25

Back at Castle Sideways, the fun park was ready! King Burt had invited everyone he knew, including the Princess of Plopp, President Daisy of Klaptrap and Duke Von Fidget. He couldn't wait to show them how good his adventure park was.

'It's much better than all of yours put together,' he boasted.

Even though it was a boast, it was also true. The place was amazing! That's what you get when you ask Pearlin to design you an adventure park.

Pearlin handed King Burt a pair of

scissors and he cut the ribbon to officially open the park.

'I declare the Squirrel Helm Realm of Wonder OPEN! WAHOO! LET'S DO THIS!'

CHAPTER 26

Meanwhile, in the woods outside Hogford, Cilla Da Spell was at home.

She woke from a strange dream. She had been riding in a cauldron while being chased by Knight Sir Louis.

The dream didn't seem to make any sense. Why would Knight Sir Louis be chasing her? She remembered the cauldron had a face too. That was odd.

She looked out of her small window to check on her moneybox on legs. It was parked safely outside. But next to it was . . . odd! A cauldron. What a coincidence! Or was it? Cilla stepped out to examine the cauldron. It was shiny and orange. Despite looking very heavy, it seemed to be floating very slightly above the ground.

'Methinks thou art the Cauldron of Chaos,' she said. 'Thou wast in the news.'

She looked from it to her moneybox on legs.

'Thou are hither to steal my money, I do suppose.' Cilla was defiant.

'Take it if thou wish,' she barked at the cauldron. 'I careth only to be the most wondrous witch ever. Money cometh and goeth. I canst easily earn more.'

'Ha, ha, ho. I know,' said a voice inside Cilla's head.

'Ods bodkins! Be that you?' said Cilla.

The Cauldron of Chaos could have taken the money box. But the truth was, the cauldron was finding it harder and harder to grab the money it wanted. People were getting wise to the cauldron and hiding their money away. That's when the cauldron had an idea. What if it could get people to just give it their money? Of their own free will?

Cilla was amazed by the cauldron's magic. 'Thou canst speak! Within mine head. Without need of sound. Forsooth, tis strange and wondrous!'

'Yes, yes. Now, listen to me,' said the cauldron. 'You are something special, Cilla Da Spell.'

This was exactly what Cilla wanted to hear. That she was special.

'Together we could be something glorious!' said the cauldron.

'What dost thou mean?'

'Come closer. Look into my cauldron.'

Cilla stepped closer, cautiously, carefully. She looked inside the cauldron. At the bottom, she could see her own face reflected. The image wibbled and wobbled and wubbled. Then it revealed a picture. She could see a mountain top. Standing there was the most powerful witch in history. She

had long, orange robes. Beneath her, people lined the mountainside and chanted.

'Cilla. Cilla. Cilla.'

'I can help you become the witch you want to be and more,' said the cauldron. 'All I desire in return is a few pennies. Here and there. Maybe some gems. Rubies. Emeralds. Diamonds.'

Cilla looked at the image inside the cauldron. She yearned to become that witch. Oh, so much!

She was still struggling with new ideas. This partnership could work in her favour, she thought. Perhaps it would unlock a whole new way of thinking . . . a whole new range of magical creations?

The cauldron was hoping for the same. It had powerful magic within it, but it wasn't the great thinker or innovator that Cilla was. She reminded the cauldron of its creator from long ago, the wizard Florin. Yes. YES! If only it could persuade her to join forces, then it could use her mind!

'What must I do?' asked Cilla.

'Just step inside my cauldron.'

'Why? Wherefore?' asked Cilla.

'Do you want to be the best witch ever or not?' said the cauldron slyly.

Cilla put her hands on the side of the cauldron. She had expected it to be cold. But it was warm, like an animal. She lifted herself up and into the cauldron's basin.

'What now?' she asked.

'Now this . . .' said the cauldron and chuckled, 'HA, HA, HO!'

Suddenly there was a flash of orange light! And then where there had been two things, there was now one. Cilla and the cauldron were one being! Cilla had vanished. The cauldron remained, but now it had a face!

CHAPTER
IS IT A BIRD?

And now a report from the Squirrel Helm UFO Society:

CHAPTER 27

Being a magic cauldron wasn't too bad, thought Cilla. For a start, she could fly. She didn't need to eat food any more. She never felt tired, or the need for sleep. And the cauldron had lots of ideas to share. It was very ancient and had seen lots of amazing sights. That meant Cilla was having new ideas again. She was thinking up new spells and potions.

Despite being physically one with the cauldron, Cilla still felt like Cilla. She could still hear her own thoughts. It was strange that she couldn't always hear the cauldron's thoughts. But maybe it didn't have many? Or maybe it was keeping secrets from her? She wasn't sure. But hey, this was an adventure, she told herself. One day, when she became tired of it, she would ask the cauldron to undo the magic. Then Cilla could have her old body back and the cauldron could go and do whatever it wanted.

Although she didn't need to eat food, she did feel hunger. But the hunger was for gems and gold and money. The cauldron had gone around stealing it and made itself very unpopular. That wasn't Cilla's way. She thought the best way was to get people to give you their money by selling them something they needed.

So, Cilla continued to make and sell her special magical products. Even better, she could now act as her own delivery service, flying around all over Squirrel Helm.

Of course, people were still looking for the thieving cauldron, so Cilla told some fibs.

AREN'T YOU THE SAME CAULDRON THAT STOLE ALL THE MONEY FROM THE BANK?

DID THAT CAULDRON HAVE A FACE?

When Cilla made money, she could tell the cauldron was content. What she didn't know was that with each coin, each gem, each jewel, the Cauldron of Chaos was becoming stronger and stronger.

Ha, ha, ho, I'm never letting this Cilla go, thought the cauldron to itself. *She'll make me richer than*

I've ever been! She is exactly what I needed. Such a good thinker. New ideas! New possibilities!

'What was that thought?' asked Cilla. 'Did thou thinkest something of me?'

'Nothing to worry about,' lied the cauldron, 'just thinking what a great team we make.'

CHAPTER 28

Louis, Catalogue and Clunkalot used their new map of Transylwoofia to find the hill of the Were-Whoodles. It was time to pick some celery!

That doesn't sound very epic, does it? But let's remember, most celery isn't magical and isn't protected by bloodthirsty creatures. And let's remember that if you were to be bitten by a Were-Whoodle, you would become one too!

DRAW YOURSELF AS A WERE WHOODLE

YOU'LL NEED..

A FLUFFY
FACE

WERE
WHOODLE
EYES

STYLISH
ROBES
(PLAIN OR PATTERN)

Louis had chosen to approach the hill in the middle of the day. Everyone knows were-creatures like the night, and especially a bright moon. It gives them power! Louis and his team waited for midday, but as they crossed over onto the bottom of the hill, something impossible happened . . . the sun went out! The sky went dark, filled with stars . . . and a bright moon appeared.

'Well, butter my trotters,' said Catalogue.

'How can it be night?' said Louis, also surprised. He'd never experienced anything like it.

'It is always night here,' said a voice, and they turned to see a large, knobbly toad sitting on a rock.

'That is making about as much sense as earwax ice cream,' said Catalogue.

'OK, it's not always night here,' agreed the toad. 'But there is a magic circle around the hill. If you cross it by day, you are frozen in time until night falls.'

'So, you're saying we've been standing here since lunchtime?' asked Louis.

'Frozen like a popsicle? Not remembering nothing?' added Catalogue.

'You've got it,' croaked the toad.

'Are you some sort of guardian? A friend of the Were-Whoodles?' asked Louis.

'Nah,' said the toad. 'I'm just waiting for someone to defeat the Were-Whoodles so I can get some of that tasty celery. Good luck!'

Louis, Catalogue and Clunkie prepared themselves. They put on their silver silk onesies.

'Let's hope these really do keep us safe from the Were-Whoodles,' said Louis.

They sneaked up the hill. Near the top was a large boulder. Louis and Catalogue hid behind it and peered out. Stalks of shiny celery pierced the soil. There was plenty to harvest. But for each stalk there was a protector. A Were-Whoodle!

Louis took out Steve Jabs.

'Sorry, Steve, but I'm going to have to use you like a gardening tool. It's time to chop some celery.'

Steve considered this and offered:

CELERY MAKES A LOVELY
SALAD WITH APPLES, MUSTARD
AND BLUE CHEESE.
TRY ADDING ALMONDS AND
PARSLEY FOR EXTRA FLAVOUR.

Louis nodded to Catalogue and Clunkie. 'OK, in three, two, one. GO!'

They jumped out from their hiding place and ran towards the celery.

Immediately, the fearsome, dreaded and very cute Were-Whoodles saw them. The creatures looked almost identical, except each one had a collar with a different nametag.

'TOUCH NOT THE CELERY OF SHOCKS!' shouted the one with the nametag that said Patrick.

'We want it for a good cause,' said Louis. 'To defeat an evil cauldron!'

'No one shall take the Celery of Shocks, EVER,' shouted another Were-Whoodle called Tommy.

'Woof woof woof,' said a third whose nametag said Tess.

Catalogue looked at the three Were-Whoodles with curiosity.

'Why is you two, Patrick and Tommy, talking and that one, Tess, is a-woofing?' asked Catalogue.

PATRICK   TOMMY   TESS

Patrick explained, 'Well I used to be Knight Sir Patrick and that's my chum Knight Sir Tommy. We went everywhere with our doggy Tess. Turns out you can turn dogs and people into Were-Whoodles. Fascinating really. Now . . . PREPARE FOR YOUR DOOM!'

CHAPTER 29

When the Were-Whoodles came closer to Louis and his friends, they sensed the silver onesies.

They hissed and shivered and wailed, 'Argh! Silver! NOOOoooo!'

'The onesies are working!' said Louis happily.

Louis worked quickly with Steve. Swish. Swash. Flick. He cut the celery and Catalogue gathered it up, throwing it inside Clunkie's metal belly.

SWISH

CHOP

This is easy, thought Louis to himself. *We're going to be out of here in no time!*

And then he noticed something odd about Catalogue's onesie. It seemed to be disappearing, a thread at a time.

Had someone cast a spell on it? Had Nobody the skeleton fooled them? No. Louis turned and saw a familiar figure sitting on top of the nearby boulder. It was the toad. He held a thread each from Clunkalot's, Catalogue's and Louis' onesies. He pulled on the threads, unspooling their protective outfits. With one final tug, the onesies fell to pieces.

'So, you are working for the Were-Whoodles after all!' shouted Louis, annoyed he had trusted the toad so easily.

'But what about the tasty celery you is wanting?' said Catalogue.

Steve Jabs spoke up, 'After the tadpole stage, frogs and toads are not vegetarian. They eat slugs, spiders and ants!'

'Right,' leered the toad. 'I don't eat celery. YUCK! But soon I'm going to try some pork chops!'

The toad looked at Catalogue and licked his lips.

'ATTACK!' shouted Tommy the Were-Whoodle.

Louis watched in terror as the Were-Whoodles rushed towards them. There was no way to defeat so many! If only he'd had his old sword, he might have been able to use Dave's magic powers to undo the Were-Whoodles' curses and turn them back into the people they once were. But then Louis' brain did what it always does when he's in a terrifying situation. It searched around inside all his thoughts for a way to survive. And that's when

Louis remembered the bag the ghosts had given him.

THIS BAG CONTAINS A COLD, SPOOKY WIND. ONCE YOU HAVE THE CELERY, OPEN THE BAG AND LET THE WIND OUT.

'Squeeze together,' Louis shouted at Catalogue and Clunkalot.

Louis sheathed Steve Jabs, grabbed the bag of wind and just before the Were-Whoodles reached them, he opened the bag.

'OOOOOOOOOOOOooooooooOOOOO OOOOoooooo,' went the wind.

And it blasted Louis, Catalogue and Clunkalot up into the air like a tornado. It carried them far across the land of Transylwoofia, over the ghostly castle, over the rocky hills, over the town of Angreemob, and over the River Sploosh. It blew them all the way back to Squirrel Helm.

At last, the ghostly wind blew itself out and they landed in a pile, laughing and cheering. They'd done it.

They had survived the Were-Whoodles and grabbed a good harvest of the Celery of Shocks.

'Come on,' said Louis. 'Let's get back to Castle Sideways. We've got a cauldron to catch!'

CHAPTER 30

Cilla was feeling bored. Just because she could work without sleeping didn't mean she wanted to do that and nothing more. When the weekend arrived, she could feel the cauldron coaxing her to go and find more treasure. The cauldron was hungry all the time. In fact, the more riches it ate, the hungrier it became. But Cilla spoke up.

'I desire a rest,' she said.

'More gold,' demanded the cauldron.

'Just for a day. Let us do something merry!' said Cilla.

The cauldron could feel Cilla's unhappiness rising. If Cilla was unhappy, she might stop making money! So, the cauldron relented.

'What do you want to do?' it asked irritably.

'Go to the Squirrel Helm Realm of Wonder! It did but open last week!'

'Realm of Wonder? What's that?' asked the cauldron.

'A theme park close by Castle Sideways! There be rides and games. It will be most thrilling!'

The cauldron didn't think it sounded thrilling, but it liked castles. Castles often had riches. Crowns. Jewels. Thrones of gold! Ha, ha, ho!

And so, Cilla Da Cauldron launched into the air and headed off for a weekend of fun.

CHAPTER 31

What was King Burt's new theme park really like?

Was it any good?

Time for a review!

Let's check in with famous thrill seeker and theme park critic, Baron Albert Snidely.

Here are Snidely's reviews for the other theme parks he has visited:

The Big Widget in the Kingdom of Proud Fidget

ONE STAR. The Big Disappointment! Was SOOO tame! Rides for babies. Awful.

Thunderclap Towers in the Republic of Klaptrap

ONE AND A HALF STARS.
More like ThunderSPLAT Towers.
Not even slightly thrilling. Rubbish.

Top of the Plopps in the Principality of Plopp

MINUS TEN STARS. Plop
is exactly what this theme park
is. TOTAL PLOPPY PLOP!

Baron Snidely was very hard to impress. Perhaps he'd have something better to say about the Squirrel Helm Realm of Wonder?

I arrived early to avoid the queues, grabbed a map and got stuck in. So . . . what do you want to know, reader? What's there? Well . . . there's a train of princely carriages. Acorn-shaped dodgems. A log flume. A unicorn carousel. Some wizardy waltzers. And a rollercoaster called The Throne that surrounds the whole park. I felt a flicker of excitement as I arrived. I felt the tiniest amount of happiness when I boarded the rollercoaster. I felt myself smile as the log flume splashed into the moat. But that was it! The Squirrel Helm Realm of Wonder is about as thrilling as a trip to a leaky dungeon on a rainy day. When, when, when will someone design an actual fun, thrilling theme park?

TWO STARS. Realm of Wonder? Not for me. Realm of Dunderheads more like it.

This sounds awful, of course. But note the two stars! That's more than he's ever given anywhere before. Also, Baron Snidely was the only person who didn't enjoy the theme park.

I COULDN'T STOP GIGGLING!

I'M COMING BACK TOMORROW!

AMAZING!

I'M TELLING ALL MY FRIENDS ABOUT IT!

I COULD LIVE HERE IT'S SO MUCH FUN!

KNIGHT SIR AUDREY

KNIGHT SIR LYLA

KNIGHT SIR ROSA

KNIGHT SIR FINTY

KNIGHT SIR NAIA

Yes, everyone else gave the theme park a solid five stars. There were smiles, giggles and screams of joy all round. As Baron Snidely left to write up his nasty review, a cauldron with a face flew in.

Cilla Da Cauldron was ready for a fun day at the fair.

HA, HA, HO!

CHAPTER 32

Pearlin was waiting at the gates of the Squirrel Helm Realm of Wonder. She loved seeing all the excited faces of people coming to have fun. Then she saw the strangest face of all. A face on a walking, talking cauldron. WHAT?

Pearlin wanted to know more.

'Wotcha,' she said happily. 'I never met a living cauldron before. You ain't the Cauldron of Chaos, are you?'

'Forsooth, nay. For I am Cilla Da Cauldron.'

'Come on, you gotta be. How many orange cauldrons are there?'

Cilla suddenly felt in the spotlight. What should she do? She hoped the cauldron might suggest something. But before she could think of anything, Pearlin carried on.

'Wait a moment. Cilla? I bet you is Cilla Da Spell, right? The one with that cool magic shop. I bet you've done some special sort of magic. Combined yourself with the Cauldron of Chaos. Taken it over. Wow. That's some top-level magic. Nice one!'

Cilla blushed. Not something a cauldron had ever done before.

'Twas the cauldron's idea,' admitted Cilla.

'I'm Pearlin. Wizard. Inventor. Wizentor. And theme park designer too, now.'

Cilla had heard of Pearlin, of course. Pearlin had helped Sir Louis save the world (quite a few times!). Usually, when Cilla met somebody new she felt her legs and feet tingle as if to say . . . let's get out of here! But now she felt something different. She felt like staying exactly where she was.

'It doth look wondrous!' said Cilla. 'I canst not wait to goeth upon the rides.'

'Thanks,' said Pearlin. 'I'm happy with it. But I do think it's missing something. Maybe if I'd had a magic buddy like you to chat ideas with . . . it could have been even better.'

'Oh,' said Cilla who knew that (a) she had never had a proper buddy and (b) the cauldron wasn't really working out as a chum and that (c) she really, really, really wanted Pearlin to be her buddy. Starting right now.

'You know what's funny?' said Pearlin. 'I ain't actually been on the rides since we opened. Let's go together. Talk magic.'

'Aye! Oh, yes. Yes, please!' said Cilla with a burst of happiness.

And in they strolled together.

CHAPTER 33

Meanwhile, the Cauldron of Chaos was keeping its thoughts secret. It didn't want Cilla to hear it thinking. So it had found a very deep, dark corner of its mind to do its brooding and scheming.

Here is an x-ray of the cauldron's deepest, darkest thoughts:

HA, HA, HO!

THERE'S MONEY TO
BE MADE IN THIS PARK.

OH, YES. LOOK AT ALL THE
PEOPLE. LOOK AT ALL THE
QUEUES FOR THINGS.

THIS IS IT!

THIS PLACE IS
A MONEY PIT!

I LOVE MONEY. DELICIOUS!

THIS THEME PARK'S TOO CUTE. URG!
CROWNS AND ACORNS. PAH!

TOO NICEY-NICE.

THAT CILLA THINKS SHE'S IN
CHARGE HERE. SHE'LL SOON
FIND OUT HOW WRONG SHE IS!

CHAPTER 34

A long time ago, in a chapter far, far away . . . some living diamonds had turned evil and were heading from a dark underground cavern up to the surface. Remember that? Good. Well . . . they're back!

AT LAST! WE HAVE MADE IT TO THE SURFACE.

TIME TO ATTACK!

ATTACK WHAT?

I DON'T KNOW. ANYTHING, I SUPPOSE.

THERE'S A BIG SORT OF BUILDING OVER THERE.

OH, YES. A CASTLE AND SOME SORT OF THEME PARK.

THAT'LL DO. WE'LL GRIND IT TO DUST WITH OUR SUPER HARD EDGES!

HEY, HAVE YOU NOTICED?

WHAT?

LOOK AT HOW LOVELY WE ARE IN THE SUNSHINE.

OH, YES. I'M SO SHINY.

ME TOO.

SO SPARKLY.

AND ME.

HEY, HEY, HEY! ENOUGH OF THAT.
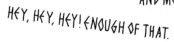

OH YES, SORRY.

READY?

SUPPOSE.

GOOD. THEN...ATTACK!
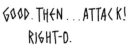
RIGHT-O.

YOU ARE LOVELY AND SHINY THOUGH.

THANKS. YOU TOO.

CHAPTER 35

Cilla and Pearlin had a great time at the theme park.

After they'd done all the rides, Pearlin showed Cilla around the castle and her laboratory.

'Forsooth, this be the most marvellous place for magic,' said Cilla. 'I do wish that I might work magic with you here one day. We could learn much, one from the other.'

Pearlin even introduced Cilla to the king.

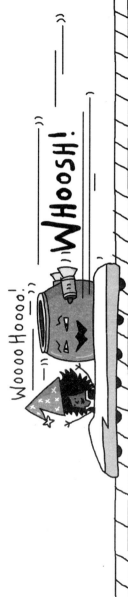

187

'I say! A cauldron with a face. Goodness! I've seen it all now. Mind you, I've met a slime monster as tall as a mountain, been imprisoned by a giant evil snowball, and spent a few days as a giant parsnip so I don't know why I'm surprised.'

Then they decided to hit the rides again, but not before Pearlin had shown Cilla the power behind the theme park.

'Here it is,' said Pearlin proudly. 'I call it the Crystal Ball of Wonder, which is kinda boring really. My friend Catalogue would probably call it the Big Blob of Fun Times. Ha!'

'Tis amazing,' said Cilla.

And then she heard another voice from deep inside her. The voice of the Cauldron of Chaos.

'Yes. Amazing. Ha, ha, ho! And just what I've been waiting for!'

Cilla felt a sudden panic as the thoughts and feelings of the naughty cauldron filled her mind. And she felt a sudden shock as though she was falling. Falling down, down, down inside a tunnel, a crack in the earth, a never-ending dark chasm. And in a way she was falling. Cilla's thoughts and feelings were falling deep inside the cauldron, until they were locked away.

Pearlin noticed the change in the cauldron's face.

'You all right, Cilla?' she asked.

'Oh, Cilla's busy,' leered the Cauldron of Chaos. 'She will be for the rest of the universe too!'

Pearlin drew her wand to strike, but the Cauldron of Chaos barged into her before she had a chance. Pearlin fell inside the cauldron and vanished!

Then the cauldron stepped towards the Crystal Ball of Wonder and smiled a very wide, very unpleasant smile.

'Time to update the theme of this theme park!' it cackled to itself. 'The Squirrel Helm Realm of Wonder is about to get spooky! Ha, ha, ho!'

CHAPTER 36

After Knight Sir Louis' successful trip to Transylwoofia, he had planned to hurry straight home to Castle Sideways. He was hoping to use his wondrous, magical Celery of Shocks on the nasty cauldron as soon as possible. Unfortunately, his return was delayed by a number of mini-quests.

There's no time to go into great detail here, but you can get a flavour of those adventures from these haiku poems written by Clunkalot:

Giant slitherer
Hunger in snake's long belly
Got knotted by us

Fly-headed knight
Buzzing for our blood and bone
Got swatted by us

Roving thorny bush
Saw us as fertiliser
Got potted by us

Vile, vicious virus
Tried to infect our noses
Got snotted by us

Compost stink monster
Yes, you guessed it, didn't you?
Got rotted by us

CHAPTER 37

Knight Sir Louis had battled his way back to Squirrel Helm. It had taken longer than it should have done. He didn't want to be mean about Steve Jabs, but the truth was, Steve was good with facts and not fights.

TODAY IS A THOOSDAY.
THE WEATHER WILL BE
EIGHTEEN DEGREES
CENTIGRADE WITH LIGHT
BREEZES FROM THE
SOUTH-EAST. SUNSET
WILL BE AT EIGHT
THIRTY-NINE.
HAVE A NICE DAY!

SAY WHAT?

Louis really missed his old sword, Dave. Dave was dependable in a battle. He wondered how Dave was doing. Had he reached Mysto? Had Mysto been able to do anything about his damaged blade? Had Dave even survived? He'd hoped to have Dave back before his next run in with the cauldron. But he couldn't wait any longer.

Louis, Catalogue, Clunkalot and Steve Jabs

were finally approaching Castle Sideways and the new theme park.

And this is what they saw . . .

- Ghost train
- Squirrel skeleton ride
- Spookycorn carousel
- Bouncy dungeon
- Creepy river rapids
- Wailing waltzers
- The Screech rollercoaster
- Cauldron dodgems

I'D SAY THE CAULDRON OF CHAOS IS RIGHT HERE!

AH NO! I'VE HAD ENOUGH OF SPOOKY-WOOKY STUFF.

CHAPTER 38

CHAPTER 39

Sure enough, the Cauldron of Chaos had taken control of the Squirrel Helm theme park. It was no longer the Squirrel Helm Realm of Wonder. Now it was the Kooky Wooky Realm of Spooky.

Visitors were welcomed at the entrance for a fee.

TWENTY BRONZE COINS PLEASE.

If you wanted to go on a ride, that was extra.

If you wanted to get off the ride, that was even more!

And if you wanted to leave the theme park, that cost most of all.

A MILLION, BILLION, SQUILLION, GANILLON, FWILLION GOLD NOTES!

BUT NO ONE'S GOT THAT. NOT EVEN ME!

THEN YOU'LL JUST HAVE TO STAY! HA, HA, HO!

BUT WHAT WILL I DO? HOW WILL I PAY FOR THE RIDES?

YOU'LL HAVE TO WORK FOR ME. OFF TO THE PANCAKE STAND YOU GO!

BUT I'VE NEVER FLIPPED A PANCAKE IN MY LIFE.

More and more people arrived at the theme park. And the Cauldron of Chaos made more and more money.

YOU'LL LEARN!

More money than it had ever made before. It congratulated itself on using Cilla's creative mind. The cauldron would never have thought of this scheme on its own. It chuckled to itself at the memory of swallowing down Cilla and Pearlin.

The cauldron could feel the power of greed coursing through it. It had never been so powerful. Never been so rich. Never been so invincible.

NOThING CAN STOP ME NOW!

'Wrong!' shouted a voice from the entrance.

The Cauldron of Chaos turned to see Knight Sir Louis waiting at the gates of the theme park.

'Because I'm back,' said Louis. 'And this time, I've got . . . celery.'

CHAPTER 40

Knight Sir Louis jumped onto Clunkalot and flew through the entrance gates.

'Attack!' he shouted and raised his sword, Steve.

'Attack?' questioned Steve, worried.

'Obviously,' said Louis.

'Perhaps consider another option,' offered Steve, 'like a friendly chat over a lemonade.'

'STEVE!' shouted Louis. 'Now is not the time.'

Louis flew over the cauldron and flicked a stick of celery inside it.

'HA! GOT YOU!' said Louis, hoping that the cauldron would be destroyed in one quick move.

But the celery bounced around inside before vanishing. It didn't seem to have any effect.

Louis chased the cauldron all over the theme park, trying his very best to chuck more celery into the cauldron's bowl.

Finally, Louis faced off against the cauldron on the Bouncy Dungeon.

He hurled his last stick of celery at the cauldron. It slam-dunked into its bowl and just like the rest, it vanished.

'HA, HA, HO!' shouted the cauldron. 'Your silly vegetable-based plan has failed, you puny, pathetic knight!'

'But the legend said you were defeated by celery,' said Louis.

'And the legend was true,' scoffed the cauldron. 'But now I am more powerful!'

The cauldron leapt towards Louis and he raised Steve Jabs in defence. The Cauldron of Chaos swallowed up Steve in one gulp.

'I want a do-over,' shouted Steve before vanishing.

Then it bashed into Louis. Louis was sent bouncing right out of the Bouncy Dungeon. Luckily Clunkalot flew up and caught him on his saddle. They retreated out of the theme park.

The Cauldron of Chaos was victorious!

THAT'S RIGHT, READER!
YOU SAW IT HAPPEN.
I WIN! END OF BOOK.

But this isn't the last page. It's not even the last chapter.

No, it isn't.

This is a book, not a pantomime.

Oh yes, it . . . whoa, there. ENOUGH! THE
END! BUT ONLY OF THIS CHAPTER!

CHAPTER 41

Knight Sir Louis flew up to Castle Sideways on his trusty steed Clunkalot. Of course, he'd hoped that a few sticks of celery might defeat the Cauldron of Chaos. But that had just been plan A.

No, for Catalogue the boar had taken a detour to the Castle Sideways kitchen store.

NOT EXACTLY THE BEST TIME FOR A SNACK!

She wasn't there to snack. She had gone there for plan B: to cook some celery. She'd boiled some celery with water until it was nice and soupy. Then she'd let the water evaporate until it was a thick, concentrated liquid. Finally, she'd gone to Matron O'Goole's medical stores and grabbed the largest syringe she could find. She'd just filled it up with the celery soup when Louis and Clunkalot appeared in the castle.

READY?

READY!

CHAPTER 42

Deep inside the dark Cauldron of Chaos, Cilla Da Spell was wishing she'd never agreed to help the horrible thing. But as she sat there, feeling sorry for herself, something strange happened.

A stick of celery fell on her from above.

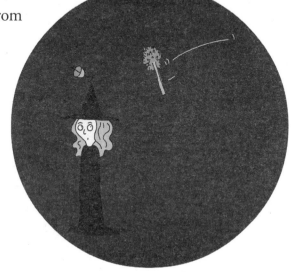

'FIE!' she said as it bounced off her hat. 'That doth hurt!'

Then another stick fell nearby. And another.

'Where doth it come from?' she wondered aloud.

'Dunno,' replied someone and Cilla looked up.

It was Pearlin. She was walking towards her, out of the limitless darkness.

'Wotcha,' she said. 'Wondered if I'd find you here.' She held up a stick of celery and said, 'I got boshed on the head with some too. And if I know my chum Sir Louis, then he's behind it. Vegetables is always getting into his adventures somehow. Evil potatoes. Freezing cucumbers. Corn-on-the-cobs.'

'Evil potatoes?'

'Yeah,' confirmed Pearlin. 'And now it's something to do with celery.'

Pearlin came and sat beside Cilla. Cilla smiled and sighed with relief.

'I am sorry and not sorry to see thou,' said Cilla. 'I am sorry that thou have been swallowed by the cauldron. The fault is most likely mine. But I am also happy to see you, for I have felt most lonely here in this strange, endless place. Before, when we played upon the rides, I did enjoy your company most richly.'

'Yeah, I had a great time too,' agreed Pearlin. 'It was nice, for once, to be able to chat about magic without boring the socks off someone.'

Another piece of celery dropped down from
above.

'What shouldst we do now?' asked Cilla.

'Well, I'm wondering if a wizard and a witch
can combine their powers,' said Pearlin, 'and
maybe use sticks of celery like wands?'

Cilla picked one up and looked at it closely.
Then she smiled.

'I believe we might try,' said Cilla.

CHAPTER 43

Cilla Da Spell and the Cauldron of Chaos were split apart once more.

'How did you get out?' barked the cauldron.

'That be thanks to my good friend, Pearlin. Now, how be it that you still have a face?' asked Cilla.

'I like it,' said the cauldron with a nasty smile. 'And, thanks to all the money you've made me, I'm more powerful than ever. INVINCIBLE!'

'Wrong!' shouted a voice from nearby.

The Cauldron of Chaos turned to see Knight Sir Louis and Catalogue.

'Because I'm back,' said Louis. 'And this time, I've got . . . celery.'

'Whoa there,' said the cauldron. 'Didn't we do this already?'

'Yeah,' agreed Catalogue, 'but last time you were dealing with celery sticks and not my extra concentrated ooper-dooper-celery-super-soup.'

'Your what . . . ?'

Catalogue decided the time for chat was over. She squirted her soup right into the cauldron. The thick, grassy green liquid arced through the air . . . and . . . and . . . and . . .

. . . and unfortunately the Cauldron of Chaos leapt into the air, out of the way, and the soup headed for the ground to go harmlessly SPLAT!

OH NO!

... but fortunately, Cilla Da Spell stepped forward with her wand of celery and waggled it around and said a few magic words.

CELERIO LEVITATUM

... and the soup flew up again, a flying stream of celery soup!

Cilla directed the soup towards the cauldron, but the cauldron flew out of the way.

'Ha, ha, ho! Can't catch me!' jeered the cauldron.

Cilla tried again. And once more the cauldron zigged and zagged out of danger.

'Silly witch!' cackled the cauldron.

Cilla tried a third time. The stream of celery soup missed again, but the tail end of it hit the cauldron's bowl.

'OOOOW!' shouted the cauldron. 'That stings!'

The cauldron flew higher to avoid it and was soon hidden behind a cloud.

Louis jumped onto Clunkalot and shouted to Cilla, 'Hop on!'

She leapt aboard, still holding her celery wand, still keeping the celery soup flying in the air.

'LET'S FLY, CLUNKIE!' said Louis.

But before Clunkalot could take off, Louis heard King Burt shouting from his pancake stand.

'OH, SIR LOUIS! HELP! HELP!'

Louis turned to see the army of living diamonds rushing towards them.

They're back! thought Louis. *And they're evil again! But how?*

Louis reached for his sword. But it

GRIND, GRIND, GRIND THEM DOWN!

wasn't there. Dave wasn't there. Steve wasn't there either.

'Oh no!'

CHAPTER 44

Any knight will tell you that winning a battle is all about timing. You must choose when to attack, when to hide, and when to run away! Timing gets tricky when you suddenly find yourself fighting two battles at once. That was the problem Louis was facing now. He had a cauldron to chase and a pile of living diamonds to defeat.

What am I going to do? thought Louis.

Winning can also be about having a stroke of good luck. And now was a very good time for that.

The sun seemed to flicker in the sky. Louis and his friends looked up. It wasn't the sun. Something big had just flown in front of it. It had a large belly, a long tail and two heads.

A double-headed dragon!

Could it be?

YES!

It was Mac n Cheese, back from the Budgie Islands. And riding on their back was . . .

DAVE THE SWORD

NEW AND IMPROVED

TOUGHER THAN EVER

SHARPEST EDGE
IN THE UNIVERSE

NEW HAT.
(LOOKS LIKE THE OLD HAT)

DAVE!

Dave leapt down and landed firmly in Louis' outstretched hand.

'Dave, is that really you?' said Louis with a huge grin.

Dave winked.

'But . . . the diamonds! They'll break you again!' said Louis, worried.

Dave smiled with confidence and shouted with some brand-new nonsense, 'EGGRADOOR! RUNGLEPAP! SKUDEE!'

'You mean, they won't break you this time?' asked Louis.

Mac n Cheese, who didn't say much, managed to say . . .

NEW!

IMPROVED!

'Then let's do this!' said Louis. 'Let's lift the curse off these diamonds for good!'

TING. CLONG. FINK.

CHAPTER 45

A short while later, the living diamonds were cured of their curse by the noble blade of Dave the sword! And this time, he was still whole and well.

'I think we need someone to come and help clean up our lake,' said one diamond.

'Yeah, every time we go for a swim, we come out evil!' agreed another.

'I'm sure we can help with that,' said Louis. 'But first, I have to fight a cauldron.'

'Going to be right tricky that,' said Catalogue.

'Cos it's gone off into the clouds and who knows where it's at!'

Louis looked up at the sky. Catalogue was right. The cauldron had escaped.

Then he looked back at the diamonds.

And had an idea.

CHAPTER 46

The living diamonds were having a whale of a time at the fun fair. Louis had suggested they try out the rides. As they flew around on the rollercoaster, spun on the waltzers and bumped on the dodgems, their glassy bodies flashed and flickered in the sunlight.

Louis gathered his friends to him. Catalogue, Clunkalot, Dave, Pearlin and now Cilla too. Cilla was still keeping the celery soup in the air. When she ran out of breath for the spell, Pearlin would take over.

'All these diamonds,' explained Louis, 'will be irresistible to that greedy cauldron!'

'How longs we going to have to wait?' wondered Catalogue.

'HA, HA, HO!' screamed a voice above her as if in answer.

It was the Cauldron of Chaos, returning!

WHOOSH

OOO! SO MANY LOVELY, TASTY DIAMONDS!

The cauldron swept down and prepared to scoop them up.

But these weren't ordinary diamonds.

They were nimble and brave and very good at jumping out of the way. Instead of falling inside the

OW! OO! SHARP! STOP THAT!

cauldron, they threw themselves at the outside.

Then Louis, riding his brave horse Clunkalot, came flying alongside the cauldron. He lifted his sword Dave and let the wind cut across his blade. Dave began to sing. And when Dave sings, it's time to put away your ears and hope your eyeballs don't pop out. Because Dave's songs are really, really bad! Everyone hates them. Everyone except walruses, of course.

OO! A BATTLE CONCERT!

SO DRAMATIC!

HE'S GOING FLAT OUT!

VERY STIRRING!

The cauldron had never heard anything like it. The sound of Dave's song echoed inside the bowl of the cauldron.

'UGH! STOP THAT!' it shouted.

Just as Louis had hoped, the living diamonds and the terrible song meant the cauldron was distracted.

'NOW!' he shouted to Cilla Da Spell.

She waved her celery wand shouting, 'CELERIO INGESTO!' and directed the soup right into the cauldron's belly!

'UGGGHHHHH!' screamed the cauldron.

The celery soup washed around inside, coating every last inch.

'I'M MELTING! . . . PROBABLY!'

And the cauldron began to shake and throb. No one could take their eyes off it. But Louis, being the smart one, didn't think it made sense to stick around.

'Everyone take cover!' shouted Louis.

His friends had the good sense to hide!

The cauldron started to spin in mid-air, and then glowed not orange, but a sort of celery green! Suddenly, all the coins and all the gems it had ever swallowed started to come bubbling and streaming out of it.

'Ahhhh, noooo! I'm losing a fortune here,' it screamed.

It went on for ages! It really had stolen an awful lot!

And then suddenly, it had nothing more. The cauldron was empty and it was just spinning and gurgling.

'I stole all that fair and square,' it muttered and then went quiet.

It stopped spinning.

And stayed in the air for a moment.

Quite still.

Then fell.

Whoosh!

And clanged into the ground.

CLANG! BONG! DUNK!

It was just a blackened, charred cauldron.
Quite ordinary looking.
And without a face.

And now the final score.

FINAL SCORE

KNIGHT SIR LOUIS **1** **0** CAULDRON OF CHAOS

HOORAH!

CHAPTER SLEEPYTIMES

Usually, Knight Sir Louis' victories were followed by a big banquet. But this time, everyone was so relieved to get out of the theme park, they just wanted to go to bed. All the visitors had a three-day sleep.

Then they had a banquet.

CHAPTER
HOW IT ALL
WORKED OUT

CASTLE SIDEWAYS AND THE SQUIRREL HELM REALM OF WONDER

The Squirrel Helm Realm of Wonder was restored, though they decided to keep the Ghost Train and a few other spooky rides. The Bouncy Dungeon also remains a favourite.

TRANSYLWOOFIA

Louis returned to Transylwoofia with Cilla, Pearlin and Catalogue. They visited Castle Spooky-Woo for a ghost-themed party joined by Sir Petrify, Dennis, Nobody and No-one. They had a great time. Then they paid a visit to the

Were-Whoodles. Cilla and Pearlin worked on a magical cure.

CILLA AND PEARLIN

Cilla and Pearlin also worked together to return the stolen riches to their rightful owners. They even found a way to purify the underground lake. No more evil living diamonds! Yay!

KING BURT

King Burt actually became quite good at making pancakes. Now, every Fryday he makes pancakes for everyone at Castle Sideways.

INSPECTOR CATALOGUE

Inspector Catalogue arrested the cauldron and put it in prison.

I IS ARRESTING YOU IN THE NAME OF THE LAWS OF THE LAND. NOW, I WANT NO FUNNY BUSINESS. HA, HA, HO!

SEE WHAT I DID THERE?

STEVE JABS

And what about Steve Jabs? Last seen being swallowed by the cauldron. What is he up to? Well, somewhere in the deepest, darkest depths of the cauldron's mind . . . Steve was rebooting.

'Hi. I'm Steve Jabs and I'm your magic sword for every occasion. I can play mood music, take great photos, and even provide directions to your next battle.'

241

CHAPTER
WITCHES (THE RETURN)

IS IT TIME FOR A STORY ABOUT US?

OO! LOOK. WE'RE BACK.

CAN'T BE. THIS IS THE LAST CHAPTER.

I DON'T MIND. I ENJOYED THE STORY

TSK! TYPICAL

ME TOO.

ACKNOWLEDGEMENTS

Thank you to publisher and editor Sir Bella Pearson, without whom these books would not exist, (or if they did, would meander around like lost ghosts). Thank you to Sir Hannah Featherstone for battling bravely against the terrors of our punctuation and sentence structure. Thank you to Sir Colyn Allsopp for wielding the wonderful, weird magic of typesetting. And to Sir Ness Wood for warding off the vampires of cover design. Thanks to Sir Gaia Banks and Sir Lucy Fawcett for supplying the living electricity to the body of our creative career.

Thank you to Evgenia and to Lucy for your love and support.

And thank you to Louis, now all grown up, for being the original audience of one.

Have you read the other stories about Knight Sir Louis?

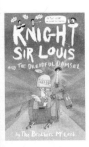    

'Sublime daftness on every page!' Jeremy Strong

Knight Sir Louis is the champion knight at Castle Sideways, and the bravest of all knights in all lands. Braver than Knight Sir Colin in the bogs of Wattasmel. Braver than Knight Sir Barbara in the mountains of Itso-Hy. Even braver than Knight Sir Gary from the soggy lands of Tippinitdown.

But Louis is modest. He says he's not brave, but just good at staying calm when everyone else is going completely bonkers.

Along with his trusty mechanical steed, Clunkalot, and mystical sword, Dave, Knight Sir Louis and his friends are always ready to do battle, break strong enchantments and defeat evil vegetables . . . all in a normal day for this brave knight. (Just don't mention wasps.)
Hooray for Knight Sir Louis!

'A masterclass in silliness!' Gary Northfield